WOLF LAWMAN

Genesis was a peaceful place which was prospering. John Fontana, a capable marshal, had no trouble preventing lawlessness until a strange unkempt group of men rode into town—and one of them was in fact Fontana's own brother. After killing, raping, and plundering, Genesis was peaceful no longer, and the men rode out of town—but there was no doubt that revenge had to be taken for all the men who had died and the women who had suffered . . .

Ray Hogan is an author who has inspired a loyal following over the years since he published his first Western novel *Ex-marshal* in 1956. Hogan was born in Willow Springs, Missouri, where his father was town marshal. At five the Hogan family moved to Albuquerque where Ray Hogan still lives in the foothills of the Sandia and Manzano mountains. His father was on the Albuquerque police force and, in later years, owned the Overland Hotel. It was while listening to his father and other old-timers tell tales from the past that Ray was inspired to recast these tales in fiction. From the beginning he did exhaustive research into the history and the people of the Old West and the walls of his study are lined with various firearms, spurs, pictures, books, and memorabilia, about all of which he can talk in dramatic detail. Among his most popular works are the series of books about Shawn Starbuck, a searcher in a quest for a lost brother, who has a clear sense of right and wrong and who is willing to stand up and be counted when it is a question of fairness or justice. His other major series is about lawman John Rye whose reputation has earned him the sobriquet The Doomsday Marshal. 'I've attempted to capture the courage and bravery of those men and women that lived out West and the dangers and problems they had to overcome,' Hogan once remarked. If his lawmen protagonists seem sometimes larger than life, it is because they are men of integrity, heroes who through grit of character and common sense are able to overcome the obstacles they encounter despite often overwhelming odds. This same grit of character can also be found in Hogan's heroines and, in *The Vengeance of Fortuna West*, Hogan wrote a gripping and totally believable account of a woman who takes up the badge and tracks the men who killed her lawman husband by ambush. No less intriguing in her way is Nellie Dupray, convicted of rustling in *The Glory Trail*. Above all, what is most impressive about Hogan's Western novels is the consistent quality with which each is crafted, the compelling depth of his characters, and his ability to juxtapose the complexities of human conflict into narratives always as intensely interesting as they are emotionally involving. His latest novel is *Soldier in Buckskin*.

WOLF LAWMAN

Ray Hogan

GUNSMOKE

This hardback edition 2004
by BBC Audiobooks Ltd
by arrangement with
Golden West Literary Agency

ISBN 0 7540 8276 8

British Library Cataloguing in Publication Data available.

Printed and bound in Great Britain by
Antony Rowe Ltd., Chippenham, Wiltshire

• 1 •

Genesis. . . . It was a good name for a town, John Fontana thought as he stood in the doorway of the marshal's office and considered the single, dusty street. And an appropriate one.

Two years old, the frame buildings were now showing the ravages of weather, but that was of minor importance; eventually their owners intended to replace the wooden structures with stone or brick, if a deposit of suitable clay could be found within a reasonable distance. What did count was that Genesis was a success insofar as its founders were concerned.

Originally the town had stood on the West Virginia side of the Ohio River at a point where almost annually the big stream rose from its banks to spread destruction and quite often death before receding. As is the way of men, the inhabitants of the little village withstood the river's onslaughts stoically, accepting the toll exacted, digging out of the mud, salvaging what they could, and burying their dead when called upon to do so. But a breaking point was finally reached.

Why stay there and face the loss so regularly imposed upon them? It was time for a fresh beginning, anyway. The war was over. The country was moving west. Why not abandon the Ohio and its merciless tithing, become a part of the hegira and start anew elsewhere?

The community discussed it for better than a year, came to a unanimous decision; it was far better to go through the pains of starting over than to yearly have all you had worked to achieve in fifty-two weeks wiped out in a single night or day.

And so the town loaded all things usable and portable onto every vehicle available and families—merchants, farmers, ordinary workers, even the local physician—headed west. They found their Promised Land in the pine-clad hills and grass-silvered flats of New Mexico, and settled there on a broad plain across which coursed what was termed a river by those already in the area but considered a creek by the newcomers.

With the sanction and blessing of territorial authority they set about erecting their town, each person taking up again his established calling, although there were a few more adventuresome souls who elected to try their hand at cattle raising, which was more in accordance with the country.

Their choice of a location proved to be fortunate, it being near one of the major east-west cross trails to Texas at one end, and the newly created Territory of Arizona on the other. Long before all of the necessary buildings, with their contained living quarters, were completed, pilgrims had begun to veer from the old path and swing by the new settlement to replenish supplies or to just break the long, monotonous journey in which they were engaging.

That was when John Fontana first heard of the new town on Willow River. At the time he was serving as marshal in Gila Bend, a so-so job that paid little but was a step in the right direction away from the uncertainties of being a hired gun, shotgun messenger, bullion wagon outrider, and other similar vocations that he had been following.

Three men had walked into his jail one fall morning, introduced themselves as Aaron Bright, Silas Galt, and Ed Roberts, merchants. They were a delegation from a place called Genesis, an up-and-coming settlement in the western part of the Territory. They were looking for a marshal, had heard of him, knew of his past and present, and wished to offer him the job. The wages quoted were double those he was receiving.

They were having no trouble, no particular problems; they simply foresaw what the future held and intended to be ready. More and more persons were passing through the town. The old trail was already forgotten, and now they were beginning to get travelers moving south from Colorado enroute to the Mexican border and other points. Was he interested?

Fontana was, and after remaining in Gila Bend until a successor could be found, he mounted his horse and made the change. Everything was as the committee had said; a clean, new, bustling town, complete even down to a jail not yet used, with an adjoining office in the front and living quarters off the rear.

He had little to do for the first few months—an occasional

theft, neighborly misunderstandings that came to blows, but business picked up sharply after several of the big cattle outfits to the south began to route their trail drives by Genesis in the interest of having supplies more readily available.

It was at that point that the Sundowner Saloon came into being. There had been no such place back on the Ohio; farmers never had time to get drunk, it was said. But here in a town placed in the center of a land where it was a full day's ride in any direction to the nearest bar, it became a necessity if outsiders and their patronage were to be accommodated.

The townspeople had nothing against drink. What a man did was his own business, and when Sid Collier presented himself and made known his desire to erect a saloon at the edge of the settlement, it was duly taken under consideration by the elders. It was granted, albeit over the objections of the Reverend Moore who captained the Methodist Church. The minister did win out on two points, however; the saloon was to remain closed on the Sabbath and was to employ no women in any capacity.

Collier readily agreed to these stipulations, and subsequently complied. Fontana never had any occasion to complain that the man was not living up to his contract.

Now, with two years and a few months behind it, Genesis could only be considered a going concern. Pleased with that thought, the lawman leaned against the doorframe of his office and let his glance travel slowly along the street.

His was the first structure at its west end on the southern side. Next to it lay the Bon Ton Café, the property of Asa Wheeler. Adjoining the restaurant was Lige Getty's New-Start Hotel, the only two-storied edifice in town. Beside it stood the broad, low-roofed general store, owned and operated by Aaron Bright.

Two small and as yet unoccupied buildings came next in line, and then a hundred-yard square of vacant land destined one day to become the town square or park, and finally, off to itself, the Sundowner.

Across from his office and jail, a bit to the west on the opposite side of the street, was Olaf Swenson's Livery Stable and Blacksmith Shop. East of it stood Galt's Feed & Seed Store, Robert's Hardware, a building that housed in one half the quarters of George J. Teague, M.D., and in the other, Mrs. Gay's Women's & Children's Clothes. Last in the row was Bill Sweitzer's Meat Market, and then another untenanted building. On beyond, where Willow River made a deep bend and trees grew in dense profusion, was Cottonwood Grove, a place where families held numerous picnics during the warm, summer evenings, and where the annual church social and other civic affairs took place.

The Reverend Moore's church—narrow, white, and thin-steepled—stood off by itself on the flat behind the hardware store. It was a fine, grassy area covered with many trees, and while businessmen still maintained living quarters for themselves and their families in the rear of their establishments, there was talk of soon building separate residences in that part of the settlement.

All in all, John Fontana reckoned he had made a good move when he accepted the job as lawman for Genesis. A minimum of trouble, better than average wages, comfortable quarters, a half a hundred persons whom he could call friends, plus many more scattered around the countryside with whom he was acquainted. It was the good life, and he thought little of the days when he lived by the gun hanging on his hip—and missed none of it.

"Mornin'."

Fontana straightened at the greeting, half turned. Asa Wheeler, squat, balding and wearing a fresh white apron, was propping back the door to his firm in preparation for the day's business.

"Coffee'll be ready in a minute," he continued, stepping out into the already hot June sunshine. "Going to be another scorcher."

"Seems," Fontana murmured. A big, muscular man, two inches above the six-foot mark and crowding two hundred pounds, he towered above the café owner. "Setting in early this year."

"Ain't no judge of that," Wheeler said. "Back home we'd a-been getting rains." He paused, eyes halting on several riders swinging into the street near Swenson's. "Customers coming."

Fontana swung his attention to the visitors. Seven men, dust-grayed and slack in their saddles. Their horses appeared to have come far—and fast. He frowned. Three looked vaguely familiar.

"Not specially the kind we want," the lawman said, considering the party narrowly as, head down and shoulders slumped, they rode past.

Wheeler sighed. "Expect you're right. Shame, though.

Thing's've been quiet this week. Could use the business. . . .
Maybe they're just stopping by, not figuring to stay over."

"What I aim to find out," Fontana said, and stepping
down into the street turned toward the Sundowner, where
the riders were pulling up to the hitchrack.

• 2 •

Fontana approached at an easy stride, showing neither haste nor reluctance. The seven men, ignoring him, mounted the saloon's steps, crossed the porch, and entered. Ordinarily Sid Collier did not open for business at such an early hour, but being Saturday, it was clean-up day and he had his swamper already on the job.

Reaching the building, the lawman paused on the gallery, let his glance rake the horses. All were pretty well used up, needed feed and rest. Raising his eyes he noted Galt out in front of his store watching him intently. Farther on Olaf Swenson had come into the open and was moving to join the seed merchant. Evidently both also had noted and now had misgivings about the early arrivals.

Nodding to them, Fontana stepped to the doorway of the Sundowner and entered. The riders were lined up at the bar. Collier, a bottle in his hand, was filling the glasses he had set before them. Off to the right old Wilce Shaeffer was indolently sweeping.

"Morning, Marshal," Collier said, looking up.

Fontana bucked his head and continued on toward the newcomers, who still gave no indication of being aware of his presence. Drawing up behind them, he studied their backs.

"Like a word with all of you," he said after a time.

The group wheeled slowly. Surprise jolted Fontana, brought a quick frown to his weather darkened features.

"*Salud,* kid," the tall one in the center said sardonically, lifting his glass.

"Bart," the lawman said coldly in acknowledgment, and let his glance travel over the others. Three of them he knew. Besides the tall one there was Shorty Reece, a squat, dour gunman, and a lean, whiplike individual with close-set darting eyes known as Bill Glade. Years before he had come up against the pair in Wichita. The others were strangers.

10

"This here badge-toter's my kid brother," Bart said condescendingly. "Sort of a black sheep of the family maybe."

All laughed. One of the riders, a spare blond man with pale eyes, whistled softly as he took in the lawman's size. "Kid!" he echoed. "Just how big does a man get down where you come from?"

Bart Fontana grinned. "Not much bigger'n him for sure," he said, and leaning forward extended his hand. "Been a mighty long time, kid."

John took his brother's fingers into his own, squeezed briefly. They had never been close, and his only recollection of their childhood together was of the bullying punishment the older, and then larger, Bart had constantly visited upon him.

"Fifteen years," he said indifferently. "Who're your friends?"

Bart half turned. He was as tall as his brother but lacked the solid weight. There was little resemblance in their features.

"Jasper on the end there's Wayne Vetch," he said, pointing at the one who had been impressed by the lawman's size. "That there's Buck Buckram, the redhead. The galoot standing next to him is Bill Glade."

"We've met," the gunman said noncommittally.

"Same here," Shorty Reece added. "Just can't remember where."

"Wichita," Fontana said.

Bart considered his brother thoughtfully, nodded. "Well, no matter. They're good boys—and they're with me." He jerked a thumb at the man slouched beside Reece. "Name's Nick Tallent, and the big'n there is Rufe Cobb."

Fontana only nodded at the introductions, did not offer his hand. When they were done he put his attention back on his brother.

"Riding through?"

Bart laughed, wagged his head at his friends. "Now, ain't that just like a lawman? We just got here and right away he goes asking if we was moving right on! Man'd figure we plain wasn't welcome!"

"You're not, if you're here to start trouble."

Bart set his glass back on the counter, motioned to Collier for a refill. "Trouble? Hell no, we ain't that kind. We're just a bunch of poor old working cowhands looking for a job. Headed for Arizona, we are."

Reece bobbed his head. "That's the truth, Marshal. Seen this town, and being mighty dry we took the notion to haul up, have ourselves a couple of drinks."

"Horses are a mite ganted, too," Tallent said. "Was even figuring we could stay the night, was it all right with you."

"Sure it's jake with him!" Bart said loudly. "He's my kid brother, ain't he? How about having a drink with us, brother?"

Fontana shrugged. He reckoned there would be no harm in the party staying over until morning—and there was truth in the contention that their horses needed rest and care. Too, Bart appeared to be more or less the leader of the bunch, and while there was little other than a common parentage between them, he would think enough of that relationship to keep the others in hand.

As for the drink, he turned to Collier, said, "Make it a short one, Sid. Bit early for me."

The saloonman procured another glass, filled it three-quarters full. The riders replenished their drinks. Shorty Reece held his aloft.

"This here's to the law!" he said, and downed its contents.

Bart gulped his liquor, slapped John on the back. "How long you been marshaling around here?"

"Couple of years, more or less."

"Might've figured you'd turn out to be a lawman," Bart said. "Heard once you was riding shotgun for some mining outfit."

"Did for a spell. Mine played out."

"You was looking for somebody special when I seen you in Wichita," Glade said meaningfully. "You collect your money for that bird?"

Fontana shrugged. Bart's eyes widened. "You mean you was a bounty hunter?"

"That he sure was," Reece said. "Seems you don't know it, but this here kid brother of yours is a real handy-andy with that hogleg he's packing."

"Do tell!" the older Fontana murmured. "No sir, I sure didn't know that."

The lawman toyed with his empty glass, twirling it absently between thumb and forefinger. "You ever go back home, see the folks?"

Bart shook his head. "Nope, never had no call to do that. Far as I know they're both dead by now."

"Ma is. Four years ago. Was closeby once and rode over to the place, saw Pa."

"He was the meanest old bastard I ever come across," Bart said, turning to his friends. "He surely was. As soon knock you winding with a piece of stove wood as say scat. . . . He ask about me?"

"No."

"Didn't figure he would. Always sort've favored you."

"He's near blind now."

Bart grinned. "Be a good time for me to go see him. Could get in a few licks I owe him. . . . This ain't much of a town you're running."

"Hasn't been here long. Bunch of people from back East started it. Growing fast."

"Could be, but it don't show no signs of it. Ain't more'n a half-dozen stores, and there's no bank. Every town I've seen that amounted to something had a bank."

"The general store handles that. When you get ready to stable your horses, the livery barn's at the other end of the street."

"Sure, but if you see the hostler tell him to take care of them."

"Hotel's back up—"

"Reckon we won't be having no use for it. We been going through a long dry spell. Like as not we'll just hang out here at your friend's until morning."

"Can't. Saloon closes at midnight."

Bart looked startled, wagged his head at the others. "Now, that's the dangdest thing I ever heard of—a saloon closing up. Your friend here tells me there ain't no women on the place, either."

"He's right. We've got a clean town."

"And you're aiming to keep it that way," Bart said, smirking. "All right, kid, we savvy. We'll be mighty good boys, all on account of you."

John Fontana pulled back from the bar. "That's the way it'll have to be if you aim to stay over. Want that understood. Behave and you're welcome. Start trouble and I'll run you out."

"My, my," Rufe Cobb said mildly. "He's a mighty rough talker for a kid brother!"

"What you call a real stem-winder of a lawman," Buckram agreed. "You sure he's your kin, Bart?"

"Reckon I am, but don't go blaming me. Had nothing to

do with it—and we'd best pay attention to him. Maybe this here is just a little two-bit dump of a town, but it's his'n and he's got his bounden duty to perform."

John Fontana remained quiet, refusing to let the sarcasm arouse his temper. When they were finished, he nodded curtly.

"All right, you've had your fun. Now, toe the mark or I'll be back for you."

"Yes, sir, kid brother—" Reece said.

"And forget that. Means nothing."

"He's telling you straight," Bart said, nodding with exaggerated seriousness. "Good lawman can't let nothing stand in the way of him doing his job."

"Believe it," Fontana said stiffly, and, wheeling, strode to the doorway.

• 3 •

Anger now stirring through him, John Fontana halted on the saloon's porch. He should have ordered Bart and his crowd to keep moving, he thought, but then he had no real reason to do so. The fact that he had no use for his brother should not enter into the matter, and as long as they started no trouble he could do nothing but countenance him and his friends. Too, as Asa Wheeler had noted, the town needed the extra business.

Shrugging, the lawman stepped down into the street and retraced his steps to the restaurant. Entering, he sought out his customary table near the window and settled down. Wheeler appeared, bringing cup and saucer in one hand and a small, granite pot of coffee in the other. Setting them before Fontana, he stepped back, arms folded.

"They staying?"

John nodded, started to fill his cup, paused as the screen door opened. Ed Roberts, in company with Galt, entered, crossed purposefully to where he sat.

"Them hardcases—" the hardware man began.

"Be here until morning," the lawman replied. "Horses are about done in."

Galt, a stump-solid, red-faced individual, rubbed at his jaw. "Pretty mean lookers. You think it's smart to let them?"

"No reason not to as long as they behave."

"Just the point. What guarantee we got they will?"

Fontana took a swallow of his coffee. "One's my brother."

The expressions of the three merchants changed at once. Roberts said, "Oh, didn't know that," and glanced about at the others. "Expect that settles it."

"Does make a difference," Galt added.

The lawman shook his head. "Not depending on that too much. First time I've seen him in quite a few years—and we never were what you'd call close. Far as I know he's all right, but I told him same as I've told a few others—I

15

won't put up with any foolishness. They get out of line, I'll run them off."

"Being your kin, I reckon he'll behave and keep the others toned down, too. Where they headed?"

"Arizona, he said. Looking for work. Cowhands."

Galt shrugged. "This time of year ranch jobs ain't hard to find."

"Don't look much like cowhands," Roberts said bluntly.

"Have to agree there," Fontana replied. "But you can't always judge a man by what he's wearing on his back. Anyway, I'll be keeping an eye on them."

"Good enough for me," Galt said, "but fellows like that make me a mite nervous."

"Goes for all of us," Roberts murmured. "Don't reckon we've got anything to worry about, however." He hesitated, glanced toward the door. "Looks like they stirred up Doc a bit, too."

Teague, a slight, graying man with spectacles pushed up on his forehead, came into the room. He was frowning deeply as he stepped up to the table.

"That bunch of toughs at Sid's—"

"Done talked it over with the marshal," Galt cut in. "Knows them—leastwise he knows one of them, his brother." He figures they mean no trouble."

"Glad to hear that," the physician said, relaxing.

Fontana smiled wryly. The town's leaders were taking considerable interest in him and how he did his job all of a sudden, it would seem. Never before had they troubled themselves to call upon him. It was because there were so many in Bart's party, he supposed, and in numbers they read a possible threat.

"I'll be watching them close, Doc," he said. "Just go on about your business, leave it to me."

Teague nodded. "Good. . . . Didn't mean to be butting in—"

"Not taking it that way. Had a talk with them when they rode in. Gave them to understand the town wouldn't put up with any foolishness."

"And they'll be gone by morning," Wheeler added, speaking for the first time.

"Fine, fine," Teague said, nodding to the café owner. "How about bringing some more cups, Asa? Think I can use some of that coffee."

Wheeler bobbed. "Sure—set down, everybody," he said and hurried away.

All but Galt pulled back chairs and settled on them. The feed store man turned for the door.

"Best I get back. Got a customer waiting. . . . I'll stop on the way, tell Bright what the situation is. Expect he's worrying plenty, too."

"Can bet on it," Roberts said with a laugh. "Customers ain't so plentiful we can let one get away."

Fontana, remembering his brother's request, stayed Galt with a raised hand. "If you see Swenson, tell him to come get their horses. They want them looked after."

The merchant nodded, moved on.

Roberts sighed. "At least Olaf'll get a little business out of them. And Sid Collier."

Wheeler reappeared with cups and a second pot of coffee and placed them on the table. "Your grub'll be ready in a minute," he said to Fontana. "Put it to frying while I was back there." He looked around the table. "Any of you gents want to eat too?"

The men wagged their heads. "Had my breakfast an hour ago," Roberts said. "One of the advantages of having a wife."

The conversation fell then into the usual pattern, one pertaining to the town's progress, the possibility of erecting more store buildings in the hope of attracting new businesses, the plans for the month-off celebration of Independence Day and who should be asked to make a speech.

Fontana's meal arrived and he became absorbed in the eating, listening only idly to what was being said, now and then being called upon to comment or give his opinion. The others finished their coffee before he was through, rose, and returned to their places of business. During his last moments at the table he saw Swenson's hostler pass by leisurely and then return shortly leading the horses that had been standing in front of the Sundowner.

Finally through, he rose, paid his check, and stepped out into the street. Several people were about, doing their shopping early in the cooler hours. Saturday ordinarily was a fairly busy time for Genesis, with homesteaders, ranchers, and local residents alike all seeming to prefer that end-of-the-week day to do their buying.

Turning, Fontana entered his office, busied himself for a time at his desk and at a few cleaning chores. Near noon he forsook the mounting heat inside the room and made his way to the saloon. It was time he looked in on their visitors.

Halting just outside, he threw his glance over the batwings into the shadowy depths of the area. Three hired hands from one of the neighboring ranches now stood at the bar. Bart and his friends had retired to a corner, were grouped around a table, playing cards. Two half empty whiskey bottles were before them but none were drunk. It would appear they were standing by their promise.

Fontana dropped back to the street without entering, made a circuit of the business houses as a matter of course, and returned to his office. He ate a light lunch at Wheeler's, then saddled his sorrel and took a swing along the outer edge of the town. With time heavy on his hands, he halted at the river, had a brief, cooling swim, and by around the middle of the afternoon was back in his chair in his office.

Later, he once more checked on Bart and the men with him, this time entering the Sundowner and treating himself to a beer. The card game was still under way in the corner.

"Any trouble?" he asked as Collier set the drink before him.

The saloonman shook his head. "Couldn't ask for better customers. Paying cash for their bottles and doing nothing more than playing penny-ante."

Later, around dark, as he stood in his office, Fontana saw Reece and Bill Glade come down the street, enter Bright's store. They made purchases of some sort, followed that by a casual tour of the town, and disappeared again into the Sundowner.

When full darkness settled in, Fontana made the first of his nightly rounds, testing the doors of the business houses that were closed, pausing to talk with the owners of those who were still open. In the process he dropped by the Sundowner, now enjoying the patronage of a dozen or more cowhands in from the surrounding area.

Three of Bart's party were slumped in their chairs, asleep. Those yet awake were continuing with their game. The lawman caught Sid Collier's eyes, lifted a brow questioningly. The saloonkeeper nodded that all was well, and John, satisfied, went on his way.

More disturbed than he cared to admit, Fontana whiled away time until near midnight, and then bent his steps once again for the saloon. If there was to be trouble it

would come now when the enforced closing of the Sundowner went into effect.

Bart and his party were the only patrons still in the building, the lawman saw as he stepped into its smoky interior.
At once his brother called out to him.

"Hey, kid, come on over, set a spell!"

Fontana shrugged off the irritation, veered toward the
corner table. Only Bart, Reece, and Rufe Cobb were awake,
and they were showing the effects of the continual drinking
in which they had indulged.

"Place is closing," he said, shaking his head at the bottle
offered him by his brother. "Wake up your friends."

Reece yawned noisily. "It midnight already?"

"It's here. You aim to put up at the hotel for the night?"

"Sure, why not?" Bart said, reaching across the table and
shaking the arm of the man he'd introduced as Buckram.
"Come on, Buck—time to hit the hay!"

The redhead stirred woozily, knocked an empty bottle to
the floor with his elbow as he straightened himself.

"We're turning in," Bart said loudly. "Dump's locking up
for the night."

The others began to rouse. Bart and Reece came to their
feet and circled the table, shaking their friends roughly.

"This here hotel, which way is it?"

At the question voiced by his brother, Fontana said, "Back
down the street, next to the general store. I'll give you a
hand."

"Ain't no need," the older Fontana replied. "They're all
growed and able to walk themselves."

The lawman stepped to the side, watched the men rise
unsteadily and turn toward the door. Sid Collier was already
turning down the lamps, and as they moved by him Bart
paused.

"We owe you anything, mister?"

The saloonman shook his head. "All square. Obliged to
you for the business."

"You're mighty welcome!"

Fontana followed the men out onto the porch, halted
there, and watched them make their uncertain, erratic way
along the hushed, deserted street. When they reached the
hotel and turned in, he glanced back at Collier and smiled
tightly.

"Didn't figure it'd be that easy."

Collier shrugged. "Was no need for worrying. About as

peaceable a bunch of customers as I've had in a long time."

"Glad to hear that. . . . Goodnight."

The lawman moved on, only faintly hearing the saloon-man's reply, the dull thunk of the door as it was being swung into place against the batwings, and locked. Everything had gone well, he thought as he turned for his own quarters. As Collier had said, he'd been foolish to worry about Bart and his friends. Despite their loose talk they had strictly observed the rules. It could be he had been misjudging his brother all those years.

• 4 •

Long before sunrise John Fontana awoke. He lay for a time on the lumpy mattress wondering what, if anything, had brought him to consciousness at such an early hour. He could hear nothing that was of unusual import—the distant barking of a dog, an owl hooting somewhere in the trees beyond Swenson's, but he had come suddenly to wakefulness, and since it was for no apparent reason, it disturbed him.

Rising, he crossed to the door of his small quarters, opened it, stood for several minutes listening into the pale darkness. . . . Nothing. Puzzled and unsatisfied, he turned back, and after dressing and shaving, built a fire in the small, two-lid combination heating and cook stove in the corner of the room that served as a kitchen.

The Bon Ton Café, like all other business firms in Genesis, did not open its doors on Sunday, the understanding among the residents being that the Sabbath was considered to be a day of rest for all and thus would remain so. There were times when it worked a hardship on travelers staying over the weekend, just as there had been emergencies that compelled Bright and some of the others to open up, but on the whole the regulation was seldom broken.

Filling the coffee pot half full of water, Fontana set it on the stove and went about the task of slicing bacon into a spider. Satisfied at the quantity, he then procured four eggs, and breaking them, added them to the slowly frying meat in a sort of omelette. When all was cooked, and the coffee had come to a boil, he sat down at the table and ate his meal, taking it direct from the skillet on the practical theory that the less dishes used, the fewer to be cleaned.

He had neglected to buy a loaf of bread the previous day, and made mental note to rectify the shortage. The half side of bacon was almost gone, too, but it would last another week, and he'd best wait a bit longer. Although he had a window cooler on the shady side of the house, fresh meat did not keep well for any length of time.

21

The meal completed, he rose, wiped the spider clean with a rag, and hung it in place on the wall. Adding more water to the coffee pot along with a handful of crushed beans, he shoved it to the back of the stove where it could simmer and be available later on in the day.

He would not be required to do any more cooking, he remembered with relish. The Sweitzers had invited him to take supper with them that evening, and a meal with the squat German and his wife and family meant endless quantities of roast beef, boiled potatoes and vegetables, hot biscuits, honey, and likely a chocolate cake, all well wetted down with homemade beer.

He always felt he could go a full week without food after an invitation to the Sweitzers and just thinking of it now would enable him to get through the day, skipping lunch, with no more than an occasional cup of coffee from his own pot.

Strapping on his gun and pulling on his hat, Fontana crossed again to the door. He stepped into the yard, paused. The pearl sky to the east was now changing to pale orange, with long fingers of light fanning out from the horizon. He watched the subtly changing panorama for a brief time, and then moved on, walking alongside the jail until he reached the street.

There was no one in sight, for most people in the town customarily slept late on Sunday mornings. Again wondering at what it could have been that aroused him, he turned right and began his round of the store buildings.

All was in order as he checked from door to door, beginning with the café and ending at Swenson's livery barn. On impulse he entered the stable, walking softly past the sleeping hostler, and made his way along the stalls until he located the horses that Bart and his friends had ridden in.

Deep in his mind he had entertained the hope they would be gone, that his brother and the others, sober after a night's rest, had elected to mount up and ride on. The possibility that it was their departure that had awakened him lent credence to the hope. Such had not been the case.

The horses were still there, so therefore Bart and his friends were still around, and whatever it was that had gotten him up was yet unexplained. He gave that more thought for a long minute there in the murky, dung-smelling stable and then moved back to the street. Whatever it was evidently was of no consequence—just the workings of his mind, he concluded, and thus dismissed it finally from his thoughts.

Crossing over, he unlocked the door of his office, warm and stuffy after being closed throughout the night. Opening also the windows, he sat down at his desk, picked up an old magazine and began to leaf through its yellowed pages. Soon he became engrossed in an article relating the trials and tribulations of an explorer lost in the heart of the African continent.

Now and then, however, he raised his glance to take in the front of the New-Start Hotel, opposite his office and down the way a short distance. Bart and his crowd should be putting in an appearance, it would seem. Likely they would head immediately for the Bon Ton in quest of breakfast— and discover it closed.

He hoped they were carrying sufficient grub in their saddlebags for a meal, supposed he could offer them his own meager kitchen facilities for use if they wished. He'd watch for them, make the suggestion.

Time dragged slowly by. He finished the account of the luckless African adventurer, began a second story purporting to be a true history of Maximillian's reign in Mexico and how Benito Juarez was able to overcome tremendous obstacles and successfully overthrow Napoleon's puppet.

The church bell began to toll, summoning the faithful to services. Fontana rose, tossed the magazine aside and walked to the door. He halted, framing himself in the opening that he came near to filling completely. Down the street he could see the various families moving toward the small, steepled building in the meadow behind Robert's.

Mrs. Gay, stiff and prim and sternly erect in a white cotton and lace dress with parasol and wide-brimmed hat to match. . . . Silas Galt with his wife and five children, all in their Sunday best. . . . Asa Wheeler, short and fat, with his equally stout mate. They had no offspring. The Ed Roberts, the Swensons, Lige Getty with his young-looking wife and attractive twin daughters who were approaching womanhood. . . . Several of the homesteaders with their active broods, some turning into the street, their spring wagons rattling in the warm hush, others more sedate in freshly dusted buggies.

He supposed he should attend the services, too. The Reverend Moore had gone out of his way to extend an invitation more than once, and with everything in town closed tight as it was, there was really no good reason why he should not.

Somehow, he just never got around to it—not that he had anything against religion. But he always felt that preachers lived in a world that could never come up to their expectations. To them all things were either black or white, and there were no intermediate shadings of gray. Fontana, who had seen both sides of the coin, knew there were times in a man's life when he must commit himself to an act totally contrary to their beliefs—perhaps even to his own.

Such moments of violence were not from choice but from necessity—and that was where the difference lay. He had argued the point on occasions with such men, gotten nowhere, they basing their contentions on the exacting laws set forth in the Bible, he maintaining that it was not possible to live passively in their world, raw and violent as it was, without resorting to the power of a six gun.

In the East, where the growing years were past and order had come to be established by the mere density of population and ever-present authority, it was different. The West one day would be the same, but until then a lawman must keep the peace not by words but with the weapon he wore —and in those all too plentiful areas where there was no law, a man must be his own.

The bell ceased its methodical, off-key clanging. The street was again empty, quiet. Fontana turned to his chair, altered course, and made his way to his quarters. Another cup of coffee would taste good.

The fire in the stove had sunk to ashes, but the cast-iron plates still held their heat, and the strong, black liquid in the pot was yet warm. He poured himself a cupful, drank it with appreciation, reached for a second helping.

The sudden crackle of gunshots coming from the far end of the street brought him around sharply.

• 5 •

For the space of a long breath John Fontana stood motionless, shocked by the unexpected and unfamiliar sound of gunshots in his town. And then he was rushing through the doorway and legging it for the street.

He could hear yelling over in the direction of the church as he reached the corner of the jail, where he stopped. A second splatter of reports split the hush. Taut, he hurried to the center of the street, threw his glance to its lower end.

A knot of men were on the porch of the Sundowner. Recognition was instantaneous. It was Bart and his party. They had apparently gone to the saloon for liquor, fully aware that it would be closed. The shooting reflected their efforts to blow open the lock securing the door. He had not seen them leave the hotel; their departure must have been by its rear exit.

The lawman broke into a run. The gang had to be stopped before they got out of hand and could do more damage. Either still drunk or ugly sober, they were in a dangerous mood and he knew he could expect trouble of the worst kind. At that moment he saw Sid Collier hurry into the street from beyond the hardware store, hand raised as if to stay any further destruction of his property.

The men turned, allowed him to gain the porch. There was a brief exchange of words. It ended abruptly when Buckram, swung his pistol as a club, knocked the saloon-keeper to the floor. Immediately Bart turned about, and raising his leg, kicked in the door.

Coldly furious, Fontana halted, drew his weapon. Pointing it upward, he fired a shot into the warming sky. The outlaws paused, swung their attention to him.

"Saloon's closed!" he yelled. "Throw down your guns and come away from there!"

Pistol still in hand, Bart said something aside to his friends and swaggered to the edge of the porch. People, abandon-

25

ing the church services, were beginning to appear along the street. Some were watching from windows, others from the passageways that lay between the buildings. Several men were trotting toward Fontana—Roberts, Aaron Bright, Wheeler, Swenson, one of the Carter boys.

Leaning against a roof support, Bart grinned. "Hell, Marshal, we're just wanting a bottle or two."

"You won't get them around here today," Fontana snapped.

Bart shook his head wonderingly. "Why, there's a plenty inside—"

"Not for sale—you know that. You were told the place would be closed. Now, all of you, drop your guns and come down here with your hands up."

Bart laughed. "Naw, I don't reckon we'll do that, kid. Me and the boys aim to do just what we please," he said, and wheeling deliberately, led the others into the saloon.

Ed Roberts swore softly. "They're meaning to hole up in there!"

"Somebody better get Sid," Swenson murmured. "Could be hurt bad."

"Wait!" Fontana raised a hand, stayed two of the men who started forward. "Best I try it."

"No, better we all go," Swenson said quickly. "All them guns still in your office rack?"

"That's what we need," young Carter declared, and pivoting hurried off to the jail.

Immediately the rest of the group followed, ignoring the lawman's plea to leave it to him. None of the townsmen had more than a casual knowledge of weapons, and they would have little chance attempting to face hardened men who lived by the gun.

He saw motion at the corner of the saloon. It was Teague. The physician had circled behind Bright's store, had come in to the Sundowner from its side in an effort to reach Collier. He would be visible from the building's windows and from the entrance if Bart and the others were watching.

Pounding feet signified the return of Roberts and the men accompanying him. Fontana gave them a quick glance; each was now armed with a shotgun or rifle. He shook his head.

"Can't let you do this," he said, swinging his attention back to Teague. The doctor had reached the porch, was now bending over Sid Collier. "Can only get yourself hurt. My job, anyway."

"Town belongs to all of us," Bright countered. "And you sure can't get them out of there alone. . . . Looks like Sid's coming to."

Teague had managed to get Collier to his feet. The saloonman, staggering uncertainly, was being helped off the porch by the physician and down to the vacant lot that separated the Sundowner from Bright's store.

"Keep low," Fontana muttered tightly as he watched. "Keep low—"

Almost in that same moment two muffled shots sounded from inside the saloon. Sid Collier pitched forward, went face down into the sun-grayed grass. Teague spun, dropped to his knees, fell beside the saloonkeeper.

"My God!" Bright cried in an awed voice. "They've killed them—shot them dead! Your brother—"

Grim, Fontana faced the men. "Want you all off the street —out of sight!"

"You going in there after them?" Carter demanded, eyes bright with excitement.

The lawman made no reply as he studied the saloon narrowly. He heard the click of metal as Carter broke the shotgun he was holding, checked its twin barrels for loads.

"I'm going with you," the boy said.

"No, you're doing what I told you to do—get off the street. Means all of you."

Fontana was barely conscious of his words, of their presence. Coldly detached, his mind centered wholly on the problem before him. . . . There was no way to approach the saloon unnoticed. With windows on all sides and doors at front and rear, he could not hope to get in close without drawing fire.

But with luck, running hard and dodging back and forth, he just might escape their bullets and make it to the wall of the building, where he would be below their guns and have protection. The odds were poor, he realized that. Bart and the men with him had made it clear where they stood. They would shoot him down, brother or not. What the hell had brought it on? Were they all crazed by liquor or was it something that just got out of hand?

Fontana didn't bother to think about it. They had gunned down both Teague and Collier, perhaps killed both. All would be aware there was no backing off now.

In the tense hush laying over the town, the lawman turned

to the men behind him. They were in a tight group, weapons ready, features intent.

"Telling you again to leave—"

Roberts' jaw was set to a stubborn angle. "We're backing you up—"

"Only get yourself killed. If you want to do something, drop back, circle the saloon. Stay out of sight and wait for my signal. Once I make it to the—"

"Hey, kid!"

At the sound of his brother's voice John Fontana swung his attention to the Sundowner. Bart, a bottle clutched in one hand, weapon in the other, was standing in the doorway.

"Me and the boys've took a fancy to your town. Aim to hang around for a spell. How about sending us over some vittles from that eating joint I seen down the street a ways?"

Bart hesitated, looked back over his shoulder into the dark interior of the building. He bobbed his head.

"Vetch says you'd best send along a couple or three women, too. We don't want to get lonesome."

Fontana took an involuntary step forward. "Forget it!" he replied, his voice trembling with the rage that filled him. "Telling you for the last time—throw down your guns and come out or—"

"Or what?"

"I'm coming in after you!"

Bart guffawed, took a swig from the bottle, and again glanced back into the saloon. "You hear that? The kid's figuring on coming in here after us. You reckon he's thinking them counter-jumping sod-busters he's got with him'll be helping?"

Shorty Reece appeared in the doorway. He was having trouble staying upright, and liquor had so thickened his tongue that it was difficult to understand his words.

"You sure better not try that, kid! This here town belongs to us now and we're keeping it till we're ready to turn it loose."

"That's for sure," Bart added, and raising his pistol fired point blank at the men in the street.

The bullet spurted dust a yard in front of Fontana. The men behind him jumped back.

"Just letting you know we're meaning everything we say," Bart shouted. "And, kid, maybe you're plenty good with

an iron, but you ain't so good you can take us by yourself—
and I don't figure you for no damn fool either. Best you
just do what you're told—rustle us up some grub and them
women."

Swenson muttered under his breath. Carter stirred angrily. "We just going to stand here taking orders from him?"

"You'll listen to me, that's what," Fontana said in a low
voice. "Make any sudden move and you'll be dead. Right
now there's probably five guns pointing at us."

Roberts sucked in his breath. "You think they'd shoot—
just murder us right out here in the open?"

"You saw what they did to Doc and Collier!" the lawman
snarled impatiently. "What makes you think they won't cut
us down, too?"

There was a long minute of silence and then Bright spoke.
"That mean you're giving in to them, doing what your
brother told you to do?"

Consciously or not, they were not letting him forget that
Bart was his brother, and underlying that fact was the subtle
implication that he was responsible for what was happening.

"May be the best way to get to them, forted up like
they are. Take three or four of us to carry the grub they
want. I could go first, get inside—"

"Wouldn't take me long to throw something together,"
Wheeler volunteered.

"About all we can do," Swenson said. "We can all do the
carrying, and instead of these here rifles and scatterguns,
have us a pistol hid inside our—"

"Not me!" Carter yelled suddenly. "I ain't crawling for
nobody," and raising the long-barreled weapon he was holding, fired both barrels at the two men on the saloon's porch.

Instantly the building erupted with the crash of guns as
the outlaws opened up. Bart and Reece, untouched by the
pellets of the short-range weapon, ducked back into the
doorway, began to add their bullets to those of their
friends.

From the corner of his eye Fontana saw Ed Roberts
stumble, go down. Swenson staggered, clutched at his arm.

"Off the street!" he yelled. "No chance out here!"

He spun, stumbled over Carter lying behind him. A lead
slug smashed into his leg, sent him to his knees. Twisting,
he fired into the open doorway of the saloon, knowing it was

useless but driven to do it anyway. Protected as they were, Bart and the others could not be reached by bullets.

"Get back!" he shouted again, and flinched as a white-hot iron seared across his cheek leaving a living, burning trail.

Wheeler fell heavily against him, knocked him sprawling into the dust. Somewhere a woman was screaming, and there were dogs barking frantically. He pushed Wheeler off his numbed leg, struggled to rise. They had to get out of the open—he and whoever was still alive—find safety between the buildings or some other closeby object. There in the street, it was a slaughter. If he—

Fontana gasped as a cloud of blackness filled with boundless pain abruptly enclosed him. For a fragment of time he continued his efforts to regain his feet, and then merciful oblivion swept over him.

• 6 •

John Fontana returned to consciousness with the mingling smells of smoke and antiseptic in his nostrils. At first he was unable to determine where he was, and then as his flagging mind cleared slightly, he realized he was inside a building, that there were others there with him. He could hear sobbing nearby and guns popping irregularly in the distance.

He seemed far away from it all, remote, removed. After a time, curious, he raised his throbbing head an inch or two and tried to understand his surroundings. It came to him slowly; he was lying on the floor of the church. A coat had been folded and placed under him as a pillow.

Ignoring the stabbing lances of pain, he tried to sit up, failed. There was a tightness to his head, no feeling at all in his left leg, only a deadness. He saw then that it was bandaged, and reaching up, touched the side of his face. There also was a bandage.

Exhausted he lay back, vaguely aware of the shadows moving about him, of the continual weeping, of the shooting that was in progress outside—in the street probably. What was happening? What had happened?

Doggedly, he mustered his scattered wits, sought to organize them. He had been in the street—with Roberts and Aaron Bright. Wheeler and Swenson had been there, too, and the Carter boy, the oldest one. Bart and his bunch—they had taken over the saloon, holed up in it. And Collier and Doc Teague—dead.

It all came back in a rush. Somebody had fired a shotgun. Bart and the others had then opened up. He remembered Roberts falling. Swenson and Wheeler, too, and Carter. Then had come his turn, after he'd already been hit once— no, twice. Evidently there had been others.

A figure loomed over him. He reached out, caught at its leg, tried to rise. "What—"

"You are all right, Marshal." It was Bill Sweitzer's

thickly accented voice. "You are fine now. You are not dead."

"The rest—Wheeler—"

"It was too bad for them. Ed Roberts was killed. So was Asa Wheeler and Billy Carter. Swenson and Bright have wounds. Doc says Aaron will not live. Others are hurt."

"Others? What others? We were the only ones—"

"It was later. Some of those who carried you and the rest here. When the shooting was done we have a parley with your brother and his men. For food to eat we were allowed to bring you to the church.

"They did not stand by their word. While the carrying was going on, they began to shoot again. Several of the men were hit, also some of the women who were helping."

The lawman swore bitterly. It was his fault. If he had forced Bart and his crowd to move on at the start, when they first rode into Genesis, it would not have happened. Now the blood of many was on his hands.

"The smoke—and that shooting—"

"They have burned the town—everything. First they rob, then the fire. They shoot at anyone they see. It is not possible to step outside this church."

Fontana tightened his grip on Sweitzer's leg, managed this time to raise himself. His senses began to swirl, the shadowy walls to spin. "Got—to be stopped," he muttered. "Got to—get—out there—"

Sweitzer bent over, pressed the lawman gently back to the floor. "You can't do it, Marshal. You are in a bad shape—and there is no use. There is nothing left of the town to save. Only the church they leave standing. For three hours it has gone on."

"Three hours!" Fontana echoed numbly. "Have I been lying here that long?"

"Yes. It is lucky that you live. Doc said the bullet that hit your head would have killed you if it had come a bit closer."

Doc. . . . Sweitzer had mentioned him earlier. He had been shot as he helped Sid Collier. Both he thought were dead.

"Doc—he's all right?"

"A wound in the arm, and then he was smart and played possum. Sid was not lucky. . . . They are like crazy men—lunatics, those outlaws! It is like the war, the raids, Quantrell and his kind!" Sweitzer paused, peered closely at the lawman. "You rest now, Marshal. It is what you need."

"No!" Fontana shouted, clawing at the German's arm, again pulling himself to a sitting position. "Got to get out there—"

Pain crashed through him in a lightning swift blow, set his brain to whirling once more. He sank slowly.

"Goddammit, I—"

"You can do nothing," Sweitzer said patiently. "You are bad hurt—and it is too late."

Fontana fought off the mist that was closing in upon him. "Send for help—send somebody—"

"We are prisoners. No one can leave. Also, where could they go? Everbody was here for church."

"The ranchers—"

"They are too far, those who are not already here. And there is no need now. Everything is lost."

The merchant freed himself from Fontana's grasp, drew himself upright. "You sleep, Marshal. I will come back."

Through dimming eyes John Fontana watched the squat, indefinite figure of the man move off into the grayness filling the room. From nearby a woman's voice said, "Aaron Bright just died."

The reply, forlorn and resigned, came slowly. "We would have done better to stay on the river. There it was all we had to worry about. Here we have outlaws—killers."

"The river killed, too."

"But only once in a while—and we could fight it."

A thin, stooped shape moved by. It was Teague, shirt-sleeves rolled to the elbows, a bandage wrapping his left forearm.

"Doc," Fontana called.

But the physician, unhearing, continued on. The lawman made no second effort to attract him. A curious lassitude had settled through him, leaving him utterly detached and barely conscious of the hammering pain in his head.

His thoughts fluttered erratically, one moment dwelling on the scene in the street where he had stood with Aaron Bright and the other townsmen, reverting next to the days when he and Bart were small boys on the family farm—Bart pushing him into the stock pond, Bart wrestling him to the ground, Bart knocking him from a tree they had climbed, breaking his arm.

Suddenly he was again riding shotgun for a stageline, then

abruptly was alone in the center of an Abilene street, a smoking pistol in his hand while an outlaw he had trailed for weeks was crumpling before him. . . . Cheyenne. . . . A dark-haired, smiling girl waving to him from the porch of a white house. Carrie—that was her name. He'd said he would return, only somehow he never did. Best that way. A man on the dodge shouldn't make plans.

. . . A room, hot and stuffy and filled with still-faced people. A man sitting behind a bench built above the floor's level. A judge, speaking, shaking his finger, and then two men wearing stars. . . . High walls that shut out the sun, shut out everything—and then the sun again, long, grass-covered flats, the towering hills, a river that sparkled as he rode along its banks. . . .

"Doc! Better come give a look!"

The voice barely registered on his hearing. He felt a hand grip his wrist, saw a misty silhouette bending over him.

"He's all right. Just drifting, sort of half conscious, half gone."

"Think he'll make it?"

"Expect so. That sucker's got the constitution of a mule. Won't be much good for a while, however."

You're wrong—I'm all right now!

Fontana tried to voice his protest but the words mysteriously wouldn't come. Pain was beginning to pound inside his head once more and he had become aware of a burning sensation on the side of his face. He raised a hand, groped for it, felt fingers close about his own and push them away.

"He gets to fooling with that bandage we'll have to tie his arms." It was Teague again. "That bullet cut a quarter-inch groove in his hide. Don't want it to start bleeding."

"I'll keep an eye on him," a woman said.

It seemed hard to breathe. It was as if a heavy weight was resting on his chest. Fontana tried to push it off, felt a fresh surge of pain. He sighed wearily, slid deeper into the black void that hovered about him.

· 7 ·

A voice, insistent and close to his ear, aroused John Fontana. He opened his eyes slowly, brought them into focus. It was Doc Teague. There was a woman beside him holding a spoon and a bowl of steaming liquid.

Raising his head, he stared at the pair blankly, and then as full consciousness came to him he sat up. Pain now was but a steady, monotonous throb confined to his temples. There was no feeling in his bandaged leg and the groove in his cheek no longer burned with such fury.

"Welcome to the world, Marshal," Teague said, brushing at the beads of sweat on his lined face. "Was beginning to think you wouldn't be coming back."

The lawman managed a wry grin. "Not my idea."

The woman—Mrs. Galt, he saw then—spooned a quantity of the liquid, pressed it to his lips. He swallowed, having some difficulty.

"Eat it all," the physician directed gruffly as he turned away. "You'll be needing it. Got to head off the fever if we can and you'll need strength. . . . Keep at him, Amy."

Mrs. Galt nodded, dipped out more of the broth. It was warm, thick, had the taste of chicken. Fontana accepted obediently until the bowl was empty.

"Obliged to you," the lawman said.

The woman, her mouth set to a stern line, nodded only slightly, and rising, moved off into the room.

He was stronger and he seemed to be thinking straight, Fontana realized, glancing around. The first he saw were the blanket-covered figures lying side by side below the church pulpit. A sense of desolation claimed him. Dead because of him. There was no other way to look at it; the fault was his.

Wearily he let his eyes drift on. There were at least two dozen persons in the church—women, children, a few men. Many wore bandages and there were three stretched out on the floor like him, being administered to. The smell of smoke

35

still filled the air but he could hear no shooting. Bart and his crowd had pulled out, he supposed, leaving the wasted town to care for its dead and wounded.

He glanced toward the doorway. Through it he could see two women working over a cookstove that had been brought in from somewhere. There were pots simmering on its surface, smoke streamers trailing up from the two lengths of black pipe attached to its firebox. It was late afternoon, he judged from the shadows, and swore softly. He'd been out cold for almost the entire day!

Impatient, angry, he pulled himself erect, tried to rise from a sitting to a standing posture. At once Teague's voice snapped at him from across the room.

"Be enough of that!"

Fontana needed no cautioning from the physician or anyone else. The flood of pain that swept through him drove him back, left him prone and gasping helplessly.

Teague, a cup of coffee in each hand, moved up and squatted beside him. "Here, try this," he said, passing one of the cups to the lawman.

Fontana took a deep swallow, nodded gratefully. Then, voice hardened by the sullen hate the previous hours had given birth to, he said, "They gone?"

The doctor nodded. "Rode off two or three hours ago."

The lawman gave that thought. Finally, "It true they burned down everything?"

"All but this church. Doubt if there's a wall still standing out there. Did a better job than a battery of artillery."

"It was my fault."

Teague's shoulders stirred. "Maybe, maybe not. An error in judgment more than anything."

Fontana let his eyes sweep the room. "Not the way they're looking at it."

"They're not seeing anything very straight. In a state of shock, most of them."

"Any more die?"

"Not since Bright. Rest of the wounded will all come out of it unless we have some bad luck. Includes you."

"I'm feeling better—still a mite dizzy. It's my leg I'm wondering about. Can't move it."

"Chance you never will," Teague said bluntly. "Bullet raised hell with the nerves and muscles, but I think you'll come out of it. Like as not you'll be limping a long time, however. Ought to be glad it didn't come down to the worst."

"Worst?"

"Amputation."

"The hell with that. What about my head?"

"Bullet grazed you, dented your skull a bit. Don't figure there's any serious concussion, just a little pressure that's causing you to be dizzy and have trouble seeing. It ought to go away. If it doesn't I'll have to go in there, relieve the pressure."

The lawman groaned. "Seems I'm in mighty poor shape."

"At least you're alive with good prospects, so be glad of that. You'll have one more reminder of this little foray— that place on your cheek. There'll likely be a scar."

A scarred cheek, a gimpy leg, a dented skull—but he was still alive, as Teague had pointed out, and that's what counted. He had to live—for but one purpose.

"Any chance of me being up and about tomorrow? Time I was doing something about those outlaws."

"None," Teague replied promptly. "Try getting on your feet and you'll fall flat on your face! We've done all that can be done about that bunch. Sent word to the U.S. marshal in Santa Fe, gave him all the details."

"It'll take three days for the message to get there, three or four more before he can make it back to here. By then—"

"By then those outlaws will be across the Mexican border and gone for good, I know."

"Not for good," Fontana said quietly. "I'm guaranteeing that right now."

The physician nodded thoughtfully, pressed his palm against the lawman's forehead. "Temperature's rising. Want you to lie back, rest."

"I'm all right," Fontana insisted stubbornly. "Were we lucky enough to wing any of Bart's bunch?"

"Who? Oh, your brother. Not far as I know. After they got that food we took to them they seemed to go wild. Full of whiskey and then some, I suppose. Started shooting at everybody and everything they saw—people, horses, even the dogs. Ran up and down the street, breaking into the stores, ransacking them. They took what they wanted, then set fire to the place.

"Bright's place was hit the hardest. Aaron had just got five thousand dollars in new twenty-dollar gold pieces from the mint. You know how folks around here like to lay their savings by in gold. Never have got over mistrusting paper."

Fontana frowned. "Knew he was getting it. Didn't know it had come."

"Guess he forgot to mention it to you. Anyway, they found it, took along all the silver and paper they could find, too. Town was a pretty good haul for them, I'd say. Sweitzer tell you about Lige Getty?"

"No."

"Expect that happened after he talked to you. Lige and his wife got to worrying about all the silverware at their place. Old family heirlooms and such—went clear back to Paul Revere and so on. He and his womenfolk decided they'd try to save it, get it out of the hotel before the outlaws set it on fire.

"Worked around through the grove and got there, all right, only they were spotted coming in. The whole bunch caught them. Clubbed Lige so bad he'll likely never have good sense again. You can guess what that gang of wild drunks did to his wife and girls."

Fontana struggled to rise, swore hoarsely. "Doc, you've got to get me on my feet! If I start now I can track down—"

"You'd never make it to your horse, much less stay in the saddle," Teague said, shaking his head as if to rid himself of his thoughts. "Know how you feel and there's nothing I'd like better than to see you ride out after those animals, but it's out of the question. Leave it to the U.S. marshal."

The heaviness was beginning to spread through John Fontana again. He brushed at his eyes seeking to relieve the burning sensation that filled them.

"Be too late time he gets here. Besides, he doesn't know them. I do—what they look like and their names."

"Can give that information to him."

"First thing they'll do is start calling themselves something else."

"Expect they will at that but you can still give him their descriptions." Teague paused, glanced across the slowly darkening room to where a child had begun to cry. "He can go on that, and the fact that there're seven of them running in a bunch—"

"They'll split up quick. Likely have already, and descriptions won't do much good. Out here men all dress pretty much the same, even look alike when they're wearing beards and mustaches."

"Yes, I guess that's so," the physician admitted, rising.

"I know them all first hand. They can change what they call themselves but they won't get by me. . . . And one was my brother. Don't forget that."

Teague made no reply, continued to stare at the sobbing child. Women were now moving about in the church, carrying pots of food, portioning it out to those sitting listlessly in the chairs or on the floor.

"I've got to go," Fontana continued in a desperate voice. "Was me that caused all this, only right that I be the one to hunt them down, make them pay. Won't help these folks much, I know, or the ones that are dead, but it'll be making it up some to them."

"Agreed," the doctor said, "but you can forget it for now. I'll do all I can but you're headed for a bout with fever. Probably last three or four days. Once I get you through that, then you can figure on being laid up for another spell."

The lawman groaned. "A spell—how long's that?"

"Well, if things go right I'd say you maybe will be able to ride in a month—only *maybe*, now. Can't promise anything for sure, but you best figure at least a month."

John Fontana closed his eyes. *A month—maybe!* It would be a cold trail he'd be starting out on. It wouldn't matter. He'd find Bart and his bunch of outlaws, track them down one by one and settle with them if it took the rest of his life.

• 8 •

The fever held John Fontana in its grip for only two days, which came as no great surprise to Doc Teague. The lawman's iron-strong physical condition, combined with a surly determination to get back on his feet, was a far more powerful medicine than any the little physician could concoct.

On the fifth day after the destruction of Genesis, Fontana sat on the edge of his improvised cot in the church, which continued to serve as hospital, hotel, and general headquarters, and dully watched the preparations for the exodus that was under way.

There would be no rebuilding of the town. Its heart was broken, its meager wealth gone, most of its leaders dead. Some of the onetime residents had already loaded what pitifully few belongings they had managed to salvage onto wagons and carriages and moved on in search of new homes. They would be starting from scratch and the future for them was bleak.

Assistance in the form of the trail hands driving cattle east had materialized, but they were of little use; a few days earlier they would have been welcomed as a God-send, now it was too late.

Late that morning a small, rawhide sort of man with iron-gray hair, hooked, veined nose, and close-set pale eyes rode into the settlement from the north. He toured the deserted, lifeless street, his sharp gaze taking in the blackened scars of what once had been buildings, then bent his course to the church where the only sign of life was visible. Dismounting, he crossed to the entrance and addressed the Reverend Moore, who happened to be standing closeby.

"Looking for Dr. Teague," he said in a raspy voice. "Sent me a note about what went on here. I'm the U.S. marshal. Name's Pearly Winnegar."

The lawman's stern, almost defiant bearing, chilled any amusement his given name might have evoked among those overhearing. Moore nodded politely, half turned, and pointed

40

to the physician inside the structure, who was engaged in adjusting the bandages clothing Lige Getty's head.

"That's him."

Winnegar touched the brim of his hat, entered, and made his way through the confusion to Teague. He again introduced himself, whereupon the medical man made a final adjustment of Getty's dressing and then led the lawman to Fontana.

"Here's the U.S. marshal, John," he said. "Name's Winnegar."

Fontana rose slowly, extended his hand. Winnegar grasped it in a firm clasp. "Glad to see you're coming along. Understood from the man who brought me that letter you were pretty bad off."

"Been shot up before. Figure to be in traveling shape in another week."

Teague snorted. "Three weeks at the earliest! Limitations even where a bull like you're concerned."

John Fontana shrugged. The pain in his head had subsided to a monotonous ache, and the crease on his cheek no longer burned, was healing well. Only the leg was still not functioning as it should, and he was a trifle weak, but he was giving neither much thought.

"Any word on those killers?" Teague asked.

Winnegar shook his head. "Had nothing to go on. Did do some telegraphing after I got your letter. All I could say was that there was seven men and one's name was Bart Fontana. Been no answers up to the time I left." The elderly lawman paused, fixed his eyes on John. "Your brother, I'm told."

Fontana said, "Yeh."

Winnegar continued to study him for a long breath. Finally, "You tell me anything about the others?"

"Can give you their names. Probably changed them by now."

"Probably. Have to use them anyway. How about descriptions?"

"Fit a lot of men," Fontana said. "Best thing is to leave this up to me. I know them on sight."

Winnegar considered that in silence, nodded. "Means you aim to go after them yourself, I take it."

"Soon as I can set a saddle."

"Be a time, according to the doctor here. Trail will be plenty cold."

"Already is. Way I see it, a couple more weeks won't make a hell of a lot of difference. . . . I'll find them."

Again the Federal man was quiet as his colorless eyes drilled into Fontana. Then, "Can see this has turned into something personal with you."

"Maybe. Was my fault it happened. Up to me to track them down, make them pay—"

"It's the law that'll make them pay."

"The law'll get its chance," Fontana said coldly. "It's going to be up to them."

"I see." Winnegar glanced idly about the disorderly room. "Means you'd as soon I'd stay out of it, leave it up to you."

"What I want."

"Not hard for me to agree. Got better'n a hundred thousand square miles to look after without taking on the job of looking for a needle in a haystack—seven needles, in fact. Not as young as I used to be either, and that's making a difference. . . . Want to get one thing straight with you, however—the law wants them alive for trying and a legal hanging. No good to us dead."

"Already told you it would be up to them."

"Let's keep it that way. . . . One being your brother, that going to make a difference?"

"None," Fontana snapped.

"All right, so be it. I don't like seeing a lawman turn wolf, but it's happened before, and in this case I reckon it's the only way. You'll be needing warrants."

"The kind that'll be good anywhere—"

"With the governor's signature on them they'll work wherever you go—except Mexico. May be good there, too, all depending who you're talking to. Some of them *Rurales* will let you go right ahead. Got enough outlaws of their own to look out for without taking in a bunch of gringos."

"When will they be ready?"

"Be a week, ten days before I can get them back to you. Doubt if you'll be ready before then."

"He won't," Teague said flatly.

Winnegar dug into his jacket, produced a fold of paper and a pencil. "The names—"

Fontana complied, heading the list with that of his brother. When all were duly recorded, the Federal man returned the list and pencil to his inside pocket, and offered his hand.

"Warrants'll be here soon as I can get them to you, Marshal. . . . Good luck."

Fontana nodded, settled back onto his cot. Impatience glowed in his eyes. It had tired him merely to stand for those few minutes. Tomorrow he'd start doing some hiking. That should build him up, bring back his strength.

"Was a terrible thing that happened here," Winnegar said, turning to Teague. "Governor told me to ask if there was anything you need or that he could do."

"Making out all right now," the physician replied. "Most of the folks have pulled out. Rest will be leaving soon."

"Not much else they can do, I reckon."

"No, they lost just about everything they owned. No choice now but move on, try to find work. Expect to do the same when the last one's gone."

"Going any place special?"

"Colorado. Plenty of mining towns up there that can use my services. I'll do all right, it's these people who have nothing but the strength in their hands and backs to depend on that I feel sorry for. Most of them spent their lives building up to what they had here, only to lose it all in a couple of hours when that drunken bunch went crazy wild."

"Been thinking about that," Winnegar said. "Way they pulled it off, I'm wondering now if it all wasn't a planned job. They could have heard about you getting that gold, and knowing you were setting out here all by yourself with no way to get help fast, they maybe had it all figured ahead."

"Possible—not that it helps any."

"Right," the lawman said, and thrust out his hand. "Well, best I start back. Long ride. Was good meeting you."

"The same," Teague replied.

Winnegar pivoted, started for the door. He slowed, came about, and retraced his steps to where Fontana sat, mulling over the idea advanced that Bart and the others had deliberately planned to rob and destroy the town.

"Was just thinking, Marshal. My time wearing this badge is up the first of the year. People in Washington have told me to find somebody to take my place. Seeing as how you're out of a job here, and assuming you run down that bunch—"

"I will, don't worry none about that."

"Figuring you get that out of the way, I was wondering if you'd be interested in the job. Be glad to recommend you."

A U.S. marshal's job. It was the peak all ordinary lawmen dreamed of—hoped for. But it was something not to be cluttering his mind now. Later, if all went well. . . .

"Obliged to you," he said. "Be pleased to talk about it someday—after I've finished this chore."

"Sure," Winnegar said agreeably. "Not hard to understand how you feel. Time like this it's the devil that owns tomorrow. Come see me when it's over."

"I'll do that," John Fontana replied, and watched the lawman wheel for the doorway.

Teague was right. It had taken a full month for Fontana to recover and regain his strength, and even then it was due mostly to the lawman's dogged, often punishing persistence and determination to get well. Day after day he forced himself through sessions of rigid exercise and periods devoted to walking, running, and swimming until finally the physician had to admit that he was fit.

The effects of the bullet that had grazed his skull disappeared entirely. The path of the one tracing across his face healed, but left a narrow, red groove that extended from a corner of his mouth, over a cheek and past the top of his ear. It would always be there, Teague said.

So also would he likely suffer a limp and occasional pain in his leg, especially when the weather was bad. None of it mattered to John Fontana; the long, tedious period of recuperation was over and he could now begin the search for the men who had brought his world down around his shoulders.

Not once since that warm, quiet Sunday when they had abruptly turned upon the town and its inhabitants to wreak death and destruction had they been out of his thoughts. He had eaten, slept, and lived with them in his mind, while hate and a savage rage built steadily inside him and the whole of his being contracted into one point of determination—track them down, make them pay.

Now, as the early morning sunlight streamed from a cloudless sky, the warrants issued by Pearly Winnegar safely stowed in a leather billfold slung from his neck, he sat quietly on his horse in the center of what once had been his town and brooded over its charred remains. He was one of the last to go. Only Doc Teague, the Gettys, and a family named Cameron were yet to leave. They would be gone before the week was out.

Shortly before, he had said his gruff farewells to them and listened to their reciprocating expressions of good luck. He accepted their words stoically and with reservation, convinced that while they wished him well there was in reality accusation in every syllable uttered, and that they would always hold him responsible for the tragedy that overtook them. They blamed him no more than he blamed himself, and while they must shoulder the burden of loss, he assumed that of guilt—and who could say which was the heavier?

After a time he roweled the sorrel horse lightly and moved on. Teague and the others would be watching, he knew, but he did not look back. That part of it was finished —only Bart and the murderers who had been with him that day counted now. The search for them was beginning, would not end until all had been brought to hand or killed—or he himself was dead.

Silver City. . . . That's where he'd go first.

• 9 •

The long ride to the mining camp went slowly; miles of open plains, of towering mountains, of deep, pine-shaded valleys and rocky flats where the July sun beat down with penetrating fierceness, and as each hour passed the immensity of the task he was undertaking became more apparent to him.

He was on a cold trail, one that could prove hopeless insofar as witnesses to the passage of the outlaws were concerned. Pilgrims come and go, many halting no more than a single night, some for even less—pausing only to get out of the heat for a few minutes and perhaps refresh themselves with a drink. Seldom did they tarry for any length of time, and those who saw them so briefly were prone to quickly forget their presence.

Thus it would be with Bart and the others. Ahead of him lay countless square miles into which they could have disappeared, a half a hundred or more trails they might have taken—and there would be few along the way who would recall their passage. But someday he would find that someone who remembered—a man, a woman, maybe a child —and from that moment he could make a true start. *Someday!* Unconsciously that word had worked its way into his calculations, but like all other qualifiers, it made no difference.

It was dark when Fontana rode into the small mining community nestled comfortably in a range of dark silver-rich mountains. Lamps were alight in the stores that lined the street, and pausing only long enough to locate the largest among many saloons, he pulled into its hitchrack and dismounted.

A dozen or more men loafing on the porch of the establishment eyed him curiously in the fashion accorded all strangers as he crossed the wide plank floor and entered the open doorway. The place was well attended, and at once a tired-faced woman in a dusty black and red dress pulled away from the bar and started toward him. Fontana waved her off and continued on to the counter, where a balding man in a stained apron was serving drinks.

"Whiskey," he said as the bartender looked at him questioningly.

The saloonman filled a shot glass, slid it toward him. "Four bits—"

Fontana gulped the strengthening liquor, dug into his pocket for a coin. "You been here long?"

"Two year, thereabouts. Own the place."

The lawman laid the money on the counter, motioned for a refill. "Looking for some friends. Would've passed through here about a month ago."

The bartender stared at him blankly. "Month ago! For Christ's sake, you think I can recollect somebody that blowed through here that far back?"

"Could be," Fontana said, shrugging. "Was seven of them in the bunch. Brother of mine was in the party."

It was hardly logical the outlaws would have split up before reaching this point—the first and only town they would encounter after leaving Genesis.

"Seven—"

"Hey, Pete, how about bringing that bottle down here?"

The saloonkeeper turned away, moved to the opposite end of the counter. Fontana sipped at his whiskey. If the bar owner, Pete he'd been called, failed to rake up a remembrance of Bart's party, he would be forced to make inquiries at all the other saloons. Silver City was in an important position; it was the point where the outlaws could have altered directions, cut east for Texas or due west for Arizona instead of continuing south as it was assumed they'd do. It was something he must know.

The lawman raised his glance. Pete, electing not to return, was standing with arms folded, listening to the talk at the end of the bar. Anger stirred Fontana. Taking up his empty glass he rapped sharply on the counter. Pete reached for the bottle, indolently retraced his steps. Still-faced, he looked at the big man.

"You want another'n?"

Fontana covered the shot glass with his palm. "First want an answer to my question," he said in a low voice.

The bartender's lips curled. "I ain't here to answer no questions. Go do your asking somewheres—"

Temper flared through John Fontana. His hand shot out,

grasped Pete by the shirt front, yanked him hard against the counter. Glasses rattled and a sudden hush fell over nearby patrons.

"I'm asking you," the lawman snarled, "and if you don't want me throwing you through that back-bar, you better start talking!"

Pete, chalk white, glanced around helplessly. A man in the center of the line farther down frowned, said, "Wait a minute now—"

Fontana, towering above everyone else, scarred face a taut, bitter mask, flung the protestor a sharp glance.

"Stay out of this," he warned, and again jerked Pete into the bar. "What about it?"

The saloonman bobbed hurriedly. "Reckon I do remember them. Was seven in the bunch, like you said."

"They still around?"

"No—"

"Where'd they head for?"

"I don't know. Ask Annie. She was fooling around with them."

"Who's Annie?"

Pete pointed at the woman in black and red, watching with interest from a nearby table.

"Get her over here."

The saloonkeeper beckoned to the woman. She rose languidly, sauntered up to the bar.

"Yeh?"

"Man here wants to know about that bunch that come in here last month—the ones that was spending them new double-eagles. You was setting with them—"

Fontana released his grip on Pete's shirtfront, eased back, anger now fading. Annie faced him questioningly.

"What about them?"

Fontana's hopes were rising. He'd struck pay-dirt on the first call. Now, if Annie could remember some of what had been said by Bart and his friends he might find himself in a position to turn a cold trail into one considerably warmer.

"How about a table—and a bottle?" he suggested.

She said, "Sure. Set down. I'll bring it."

The lawman moved to the corner off the end of the bar where there was no traffic and settled onto a chair. Annie returned with glasses and a full quart of whiskey, placed them on the table, and sat down opposite him. Elsewhere the saloon had resumed its normal tenor.

"Pretty hard to forget that bunch," she said, uncorking the bottle and filling the glasses. "Was throwing money around like it was going out of style. Brand new, shiny double-eagles."

It hadn't occurred to Fontana before, but the bright new gold coins the outlaws had taken likely would prove to be the key that would unlock many memories.

"Heard they were well fixed," he said drily, and lifted his glass. *"Salud!"*

He watched her down her drink. Then, "You happen to know which way they went when they rode out of here?"

Annie frowned, helped herself to another shot of the liquor. "Was some arguing going on about that, seems. There was one tall jasper. Called Bart, I think. He was for going to Texas, someplace. Don't remember just where. Two or three others was hollering for Mexico. Claimed that was the best place to go. Never did know what made it the best 'cepting maybe it was because they'd be plenty rich down there with all that gold they was sporting."

"What did they decide?"

"Don't think they ever did—for sure, anyway. Was still jawing about it when they left me."

Fontana considered that thoughtfully. "How long did they hang around here?"

"Couple of days. . . . Say, you ain't the law, are you?"

He avoided the question. "The tall one—Bart. He's my brother. Trying to catch up with him."

Annie nodded, satisfied, and poured another drink. "Was the big one I sort've liked. They called him Rufe."

Fontana was only half listening. The outlaws hadn't held much fear of pursuit, he realized, which confirmed his earlier belief. Thinking that he and all the others in Genesis who had seen them close enough to make an identification were dead, and reassured by the fact of the town's isolated location, they had taken it easy and enjoyed themselves. That knowledge made the cold trail he was pursuing somewhat less formidable.

"You never did say where they were headed when they left."

"Lordsburg. Know that for sure because Rufe asked me what the name of the big saloon there was—and did I know any of the girls."

South. . . . They had continued on south. "You tell him?"

"Yeh, the Eagle," Annie replied, once more filling her

glass. "He can rustle up his own girl." Tossing off the drink, she leaned back, considered him appreciatively. "You staying over the night?"

"Reckon so. Been a long day. How far's Lordsburg?"

"Forty, fifty miles. Kind of a long ride in the dark."

John Fontana agreed mentally. He could go on, of course, reach the town in the early morning hours, but like as not he'd find everything closed—and he was tired, in need of a good meal and a bed. His strength, he was finding out, wasn't all he'd assumed it to be. It would be smart to spend the night, or most of it, there in Silver City, rest up from the two days on the trail he'd spent coming from Genesis, and get an early start in the morning.

"Guess I'll stick around," he said. "Know where I can get some supper and a bed?"

"With or without?" Annie said, arching her brows.

"With or without what?"

"Me."

John Fontana grinned, shook his head. "Without," he replied. "Got some serious thinking to do."

• 10 •

Fontana rode into Lordsburg around mid-morning, oblivious to everything pertaining to the settlement except the Eagle Saloon, which he located at once. Pulling up at the rack, he swung from the saddle, tied the sorrel gelding, and entered the low-roofed building.

There was only one customer at the bar, an aged, yellow-bearded individual who looked to be a miner, but at a table nearby four men lounged about a bottle of liquor and engaged in desultory conversation.

The lawman halted at the short counter, and at the bartender's question made a slight motion with his hand.

"Nothing right now. Looking for information."

The man behind the counter drew back, crossed his arms. "Hard liquor's what we've got here."

Fontana smiled bleakly. Bartenders were all alike. "Seven men. Would have come in about a month ago from Silver City. You remember them?"

The man's expression altered. He shrugged. "Better ask the boss—Henry Daws. That's him setting there at the table —the one in the checkered vest."

Fontana turned his attention to the men. Daws was well-dressed, fancied a cigar, and toyed continually with a bear's tooth suspended from the watch chain looped across his middle. Pushing away from the bar, the lawman crossed to the table, and calling Daws by name, repeated his question.

The saloonman studied him lazily. Those with him leaned back in their chairs, also gave Fontana thorough consideration.

"Who's wanting to know?" Daws asked finally.

"Name's Fontana."

"You got a special reason for asking?"

"One's my brother."

Daws digested that slowly, shook his head. "Nope, don't think they ever was around here."

"Were headed for the Eagle Saloon when they left Silver

51

City," Fontana said in a carefully quiet voice. "This is the Eagle Saloon. Maybe the names'll spark your memory. Fontana, Vetch, Buckram, Glade, Cobb, Tallent, Shorty Reece."

Daws blew gently on the tip of his cigar. "Never heard of them."

"Could be calling themselves something else—"

"Say, friend," the heavily built man sitting at the saloonkeeper's right cut in, "you deaf? Mr. Daws says he don't remember them. Ain't that plain enough for you?"

The lawman ignored the interruption, pressed back the anger beginning to stir through him. "Would have been spending gold double-eagles. New ones."

The quick break in Henry Daws' eyes gave it away. He hesitated, cigar poised, thick lips parted, and then once again he wagged his head.

"No, ain't been around here."

Fontana's shoulders came forward. His eyes flamed. "You're a goddamned liar—"

In that same instant the husky man siding Davis kicked back his chair, lunged at the lawman. Fontana rocked away, avoiding the spread, sausagelike fingers reaching for him, backhanded the puncher hard across the face.

The others came to their feet in a rush. Fontana snatched up the chair in front of him, smashed it over the head of the one nearest, then staggered as a fist caught him on the jaw. Suddenly raging, he wheeled, picked up a second chair, and swinging it as a flail, mercilessly hammered the two remaining punchers to the floor.

Tossing the splintered wreckage aside, he swung to Daws. The saloonman had gotten hastily to his feet, stepped back. His hand was resting tentatively on the pearl handles of the gun he wore.

"Don't," the lawman warned in a strained voice. "I'll kill you. . . . Goes for you, too," he added, flicking a glance at the bartender.

He was breathing hard for wind. The brief fight had been a furious one and it had taken much out of him, reminded him again that he was not yet fully recovered from the wounds sustained at the hands of the outlaws in Genesis.

"Now—about that bunch," he said, circling slowly toward Daws. "Want to know if they're still here. If not, where'd they go?"

The saloonman, strangely calm for the moment, stared at

Fontana. A warning clanged deep inside the lawman. He looked quickly toward the panel of mirrors on the wall beyond the bar, had a fleeting glimpse of a man closing in on him from the rear. A pistol, butt first, was raised in his hand.

Fontana ducked, spun. His knotted fist came from his heels, traveled the full distance to shoulder height. The blow struck the oncoming man on the side of his head, knocked him sprawling into a circle of tables and chairs. Only then did Fontana see the star that glinted dully on the fellow's vest. He stared at it for a moment, shook his head uncaring, and turned again to Daws.

"About out of patience," he said. "Best you speak up— while you're still able."

One of the punchers on the floor near Daws stirred, pulled himself to a stiting position, dazedly rubbed at his bloodied head. The lawman shot him a warning look. At once the rider sank back.

"I'm waiting—"

The saloonkeeper bobbed nervously. "They was here. Hung around a couple of days. . . . Don't like to be telling on folks. Ain't good for business and sometimes it means a lot of trouble."

"You'll be in worse if you don't keep talking."

"Sure . . . sure. Well, they wasn't calling themselves what you claim."

They had changed their names as he had suspected they would do. Likely they had come to that decision and laid plans for the future during the ride from Silver City. It would make the search more difficult but far from impossible; it was clear now the magic word was gold—new twenty-dollar gold pieces.

"Where'd they head for when they left here?"

A faint smile pulled at the corners of the saloonman's mouth, widened as a voice behind Fontana sounded harshly.

"Don't move! I've got a forty-five aimed at your backbone."

The town lawman again. John Fontana swore quietly, raised his hands, hearing the scrape of boot heels as the lawman edged in close, feeling the sudden loss of weight on his hip as his weapon was lifted from its holster.

"You're in trouble, mister," the lawman growled through clenched teeth as he circled around to Daws' side.

Fontana shrugged indifferently. *Marshal,* the black letters on the star the lawman wore read. He was young, early twenties probably, had a full mustache and small, black eyes. He stood for a few moments glancing about at the shattered chairs, the overturned tables, the three punchers now pulling themselves unsteadily erect.

"Who started this ruckus?"

"Him!" Daws said promptly. "Come busting in here raising hell. My boys tried to stop him—"

"He's lying," Fontana broke in coldly. "Was asking for information."

"Information," the marshal echoed, still looking around. "What kind of information?"

"Wanted to know about them jaspers that was in here a while back—ones with them new double-eagles, Otey. You recollect."

The lawman nodded, touched the side of his face where Fontana's fist had connected. It was beginning to swell. "Sure I remember. Jugged three of them, didn't I? What about it?"

Fontana lowered his arms as Otey holstered his weapon. "Trying to find them—one's my brother." He didn't particularly like the idea of using the relationship as a pry, but by so doing he avoided a great deal of explanation. A man seeking his brother was reason enough in itself and called for no further details.

"Been smart to 've come to me," the marshal said stiffly. "Could've told you they'd been here and gone. That'd saved all this mess."

"Girl in Silver City told me they were coming here, to the Eagle Saloon. You know where they are now?"

"Tucson, far as I know—leastwise part of them went there. The three I cooled off lit out for El Paso when I turned them loose."

Tucson. . . . El Paso. . . . So they had split up. It would not be quite so easy now. Seven men in a party were more noticeable than three or four, but he still had the new double-eagles to use as an identification. . . . Tucson was nearer. He'd go there first.

"Obliged to you, Marshal," he said, abruptly reaching out and plucking his pistol from the lawman's belt and dropping it into his holster. "I'll be riding on. Real sorry about the to-do."

Otey stood motionless, surprised. Henry Daws frowned.

"Now, wait a damned minute! Who's paying for this here damage to my place?"

"You are," Fontana replied as he turned away. "Was you that started it."

"The hell—"

"Best you forget it," Fontana heard the lawman say as he moved toward the doorway. "Ain't no sense in there being a killing over a couple of chairs—and that's what there'll be if you push that big galoot too far."

John Fontana smiled wryly as he pushed through the batwings into the open. *A wolf*, Pearly Winnegar had called him. He didn't care much for the title but if that was what it took to get the job done he reckoned he could bear up under it.

Reaching the sorrel, he swung onto the saddle and followed the main street to where it forked. Noting a sign with the single word TUCSON on its right branch, he veered onto it, settled himself in the leather for what he suspected would be a long, hot ride—three, perhaps four days at the least. But he was prepared. He had grub enough in his saddlebags to get by, and likely he'd come onto a few ranches, possible even a small town or two where he could buy a meal.

Tucson, of course, was a gamble. He realized that, but then the entire search was a gamble. He had little to go on, even less now that the outlaws had split up and changed their names. He'd had some luck. They had stopped in Silver City, later in Lordsburg, after which four had ridden on to Tucson, three to El Paso. But that was a month ago; there was no assurance they could still be found there.

He glanced ahead. The trail cut down into a steep-walled canyon, was hemmed in on both sides with chaparral, rabbit brush, buckbrier, and other rank growth. He could be entering Apache country. Best he keep a sharp lookout.

Movement on the road below him drew his attention. He slowed the gelding, shaded his eyes for a better look. Two riders—not Indians. Fontana breathed easier, and then frowned. There was something familiar about the pair. On impulse he abruptly wheeled his horse off into the underbrush, spurred forward a few yards to where he'd have a good view of the men when they passed. It was only a hunch but maybe—just maybe—

Motionless, he waited in the steadily rising heat, ears attuned to the buzzing and clacking of insects in the foliage around him. A whip-tailed lizard appeared, halted on a rock, and observed him with beady intent for a brief time and then scuttled off into the dry leaves and loose rock. High overhead a broad-winged golden eagle soared lazily.

The dull thud of hooves reached Fontana. He leaned forward, straining for a look at the riders through the tangle of brush. They drew closer, came abreast, silent and features set as they rode. A gust of near uncontrollable anger swept the lawman.

It was Tallent and Bill Glade.

• 11 •

Trembling, Fontana fought back the urge to rush into the open, draw his gun, and empty it into the two killers. U.S. Marshal Winnegar, knowing only too well that just such a moment would come, had warned him against it.

He shook his head, and taut, allowed the pair to pass on while within him the soaring anger settled down into a grim sort of satisfaction. Luck was running with him. He had two of the outlaws.

After a time he guided the sorrel back onto the road and swung in behind Tallent and Glade, now a hundred yards or so ahead. He'd hang back, let them ride on in to Lordsburg, he decided, coldly calculating. Once there he'd confront them; to do so now meant shepherding them for the rest of the way, being alert all the while for tricks—possibly even losing one or both.

Keeping the gelding in check, he followed at a leisurely pace, and when they entered the settlement and swung into the rack at the Eagle, he drew to a halt on the opposite side of the street. Tense, but utterly cool, he stepped from the saddle as the pair stretched, yawned, wrapped the leathers around the bar, and then with some comment from Tallent, started for the saloon's porch. Nearby two men on a short strip of board sidewalk, noting Fontana's intense bearing and suspecting that something was about to take place, halted to watch.

Glade had allowed his beard to grow, wore a new shirt and hat. Nick Tallent appeared the same except for the fancy boots he now sported. The lawman moved silently to the center of the street, dropped his arms to his sides.

"Tallent—Glade!" he called in a tight, husky voice. "You're under arrest!"

Both men whirled. Glade's jaw sagged and then his hand swept down. Fontana drew, fired fast—too fast. The bullet smashed high into the outlaw's arm. The lawman triggered again. Glade staggered, clutched at his chest. Nick Tallent,

57

momentarily frozen by surprise, rocked forward. His hand came up, bright sunlight glinting off the weapon in his hand. Fontana pressed off a third shot. Tallent buckled, fell back onto the saloon's steps.

As the layers of smoke about him began to drift off, John Fontana methodically reloaded his pistol, and moving slowly, walked to where the outlaws lay. People, attracted by the shooting, were running into the street; Henry Daws, accompanied by his bartender and two of the men the lawman had encountered earlier, now stood on the Eagle's porch.

Down the way a voice shouted: "Somebody get Otey! There's been a killing!"

Oblivious to it all, utterly cold, Fontana halted beside Bill Glade. Reaching down he caught the outlaw by the shoulder, rolled him to his back. He was dead. The second bullet had struck him in the heart.

The lawman swore silently as he turned to Tallent. While it was of no real concern to him, he would as soon have taken the pair alive on the chance he could force them to tell him the whereabouts of the remaining members of the gang. Now the opportunity was gone.

Tallent's head lay upon the bottom step. Hunkering, Fontana took the chin between thumb and fingers, tipped the man's face upward. The eyes opened. The outlaw was still alive—but not for long. The lawman's hopes rose as he bent lower.

"You're dying, Nick. Tell me one thing—where's Bart and the others?"

Tallent's lips pulled into a sneer. "Go to hell," he muttered.

The thud of boots rushing up brought Fontana's attention about. It was the Lordsburg marshal. His features were flushed, angry.

"What's going on here?" he demanded as he drew in close.

Fontana turned back to Tallent. "Bill's dead and you're not far from it," he said. "You can do one good thing before you're gone, tell me where they are."

The outlaw's eyes fluttered, his mouth sagged. "Phoenix," he said, and went limp.

Fontana came erect slowly. Immediately the Lordsburg lawman seized his arm, jabbed the barrel of his pistol into the back of the man towering over him.

"What the goddamn hell you mean, riding in here, shooting up the place?"

"Phoenix," Fontana repeated, making no effort to raise his arms or reply. "That around here somewhere?"

"Little town over in Arizona Territory," someone in the crowd volunteered.

"Ain't much of a one," another voice added. "Bet there ain't a hundred people in the whole valley."

"How far?" Fontana asked, continuing to ignore the gun pressing into his body.

"Maybe four days riding if—"

"I'm talking to you!" Otey shouted as if suddenly remembering his position. "If you think you can come into my town, start shooting and killing—"

"One of them drawed first, Marshal." It was the taller of the two men who had paused to watch. "Me and Amos seen it all. The big fellow here, he sung out—"

"Makes no difference! I won't have no gunslingers coming in here and—" The marshal paused, looked more closely at Tallent and then at Glade. "Ain't them two of that bunch you was hunting for?"

Fontana nodded, turned, pushing the lawman's weapon aside. The swelling on the young marshal's jaw was now complete and had taken on a dark discoloration.

"Put that iron away," Fontana said, unbuttoning the front of his shirt. Reaching in, he drew forth the leather folder, opened it, and thumbing through the papers, selected the appropriate warrants.

"Write DEAD on these and mail them to the U.S. marshal in Santa Fe," he said, handing the sheets to Otey, and then softening the blunt request, added, "I'll take it as a favor."

Otey holstered his weapon, and frowning, inspected the warrants. After a moment he looked up. "You're some kind of a lawman! Why the hell didn't you say so in the first place? Would've give you some help."

"Don't want any."

Otey nodded slowly, his small eyes fixed speculatively on the big lawman's grim, set features. "This what you're figuring for the rest of that bunch?"

"If it's what it takes. All the same to me."

Again the younger man nodded. "Seems you're taking these here warrants as a hunting license." There was a note of scorn in his tone.

"They'll get their chance to give up, same as these two had," Fontana replied coolly. "Choice'll be theirs."

"One's your brother. That go for him too?"

"Him, same as the others."

Someone in the still accumulating crowd whistled, either in awe or shock, there was no way of knowing which.

"I see," the young marshal said. "Well, mister, I'd hate to be wearing your boots when this is all over."

John Fontana's broad shoulders stirred slightly. "Just keep hoping you never have to," he said. "You got any more business with me?"

"Reckon not unless you're wanting something done with their belongings."

"Use the money to bury them with. Folks they took it from are mostly all dead and won't need it. If there's any big amount left over, send it along to Santa Fe, too. The marshal 'll know what to do with it."

Otey bobbed, almost friendly now that indignation and anger had dissipated.

"How do I get on the road to this Phoenix?"

"Take the fork that heads for Tucson," the marshal said. "Be another fork about twenty miles on. Follow it. . . . You leaving now?"

"Now," Fontana answered, and turned to his horse.

• 12 •

On the third day out of Lordsburg, Fontana ran out of water. He was in a burning land of gaunt, grotesque cactus, green-trunked paloverde trees, mesquite, and little else. Once he encountered a small herd of wild burros that galloped madly off when they saw him, which was in direct contrast to his encounter with a band of peccaries. The wiry little pigs stood their ground, fiercely clicking their tusks and pawing the hot sand as he passed.

Some time later he spotted a party of Indians and immediately turned the suffering sorrel into a deep wash and thus avoided them. Other than the braves, riding south, he saw no other human beings.

He endured it all philosophically, considered it a part of the task that faced him, a phase that would pass as did all disagreeable things. He would reach Phoenix, settle with whichever of the outlaws were there, and move on. It was as simple as that.

On the morning of the fourth day he found himself riding parallel to a range of glistening, heat-blistered mountains while a pitiless sun blazed down upon him from a cloudless sky. Just as he was reaching the point when he doubted whether he or the gelding could go much farther, he came to a small creek. It was barely running, with a six-inch ribbon of water, but he was able to slake his thirst and that of the sorrel, and later continued on in a somewhat better condition.

It was salvation, he realized, for the nearer he drew to the shining black hills the more intense the heat became. Nothing stirred in this universe of flame except a dozen or so buzzards wheeling soundlessly in the charged atmosphere overhead as they maintained a death watch over some luckless creature below in the savagely efficient way of nature.

He reckoned he was some sort of scavenger, prowling the country, removing from its face the carrion that plagued humanity—carrion such as Bart and his crowd. It was his job just as the destroying of rotting carcasses was the appointed task of the great ugly birds soaring patiently in the sky above. And he would perform his chore, permitting nothing to stand in the way, as would they.

He was now well up the ladder to the successful conclusion of his task. Two of the outlaws accounted for, gone to where they could never again bring trouble and grief to others. It was unfortunate the pair had chosen to go for their guns rather than surrender. Questioning them could have brought out information that would make the search for all of the remaining killers easier and less time-consuming.

But it hadn't worked out that way and he guessed he could understand; a rope awaited each should he give up, and gambling on being able to draw first offered better odds than the scaffold.

All hadn't been lost, however. Tallent had come through in his last moments of life to name Phoenix as the place where at least two of the gang were living. It was a break for Fontana; he had thought the four who had continued westward from Lordsburg would be found in Tucson.

Now it was clear that going there would have been a waste of time and effort. Evidently instead of heading for the old mission town, they had swung off the road leading to it and continued on to Phoenix. At that point something had occurred and Tallent and Bill Glade had decided to pull out, return to Lordsburg—possibly intending to push on for El Paso, where they would rejoin the three members of the party who had reportedly gone there.

It had been a stroke of good fortune and sheer coincidence that he had encountered them on their return trip. That his luck still held was heartening; it could only augur well for the balance of the search.

Near dark, with the slanting rays of the sun no less hot than at mid-day, John Fontana halted at the rim of a long valley and stared ahead at a cluster of trees and low-roofed shacks huddled in the center of seemingly endless fields of hay. The scorched mountains were behind him now, and except for the tiny oasis with its green flats and narrow ditches sparkling with water there was nothing before him but limitless desert.

Brushing at the sweat blanketing his face and misting his eyes, Fontana considered the collection of poor structures morosely. Could this be Phoenix? If so, what would bring the outlaws to such a forsaken place? There appeared to be no business houses, no inn or hotel, no saloon—only a few mean dwellings in an area evidently devoted wholly to the growing of hay.

If there had been ranches or mines he could understand their choosing this isolated village, but he had seen no signs of either around the town, if it could be called that.

A deep suspicion growing within him, Fontana urged the weary sorrel on, riding along a faint, almost indistinguishable trail that led to the largest of the few huts. As he entered the yard a sun-blackened, wrinkled man stepped into the open.

"Howdy," he greeted, mopping his moist face with a bandana. "Step down."

The lawman came off the saddle stiffly. He was soaked with sweat, bone tired, hungry, and patience was no part of him.

"This Phoenix?"

"What it's called. Where you headed?"

"Here," Fontana replied wearily as he glanced about. "This all there is to the place?"

The man nodded. "There's a store down in them trees," he said, pointing. "Sells whiskey, too, if you're of a mind to drink. Name's Cartwright."

"Fontana," the lawman said, extending his hand. "Looking for some . . . friends. Heard they'd be here."

Cartwright's wrinkled brow tightened. Again he swabbed with the bandana. There was a stickiness in the overheated air, produced no doubt by the many water-filled canals Fontana could see threading the fields.

"Ain't nobody here now that ain't been around for two, maybe three years."

The suspicion within the lawman solidified, but he continued. "Would have been four men. Might have ridden in about a month ago. Two of them pulled out a short time back for Lordsburg. Was told the others were still here."

"Somebody told you wrong, Fontana," the old man said. "Hell, 'cepting you, there ain't been a stranger by here in months."

The lawman looked away wearily. Tallent had lied, had given him a false lead out of spite. He should have known his luck wouldn't be that good. . . . Four days lost getting there, four more wasted on a return trip unless there was a direct route to Tucson that would obviate the necessity for doubling back to Lordsburg.

"Might as well stay over a spell," Cartwright said cheerfully. "You're looking mighty beat. Horse of your'n's in the same shape. Heat sure is hell this time of year—but it still ain't bad as it'll be next month."

Fontana hesitated. The sooner he got back on the trail, resumed the search, the better, but the sorrel was in need of rest and decent feed—and the day was growing late. As for himself he would prefer to continue; a bite to eat, a canteen full of fresh water, and he'd be ready to go. Time was his relentless enemy, one that gave no quarter, and he felt he could afford no wasting of it.

"Can't offer much," Cartwright said. "Good cooking, howsomever. Got me a Papago squaw. Turns out a right tasty stew."

"Obliged to you," the lawman said. He would stay the night, let the sorrel rest, take it easy himself. "Don't want to be any trouble."

"Trouble!" Cartwright snorted. "Pleasures me a plenty! Gets powerful lonesome around here with nobody much to jaw with. . . . Can put your horse in that lean-to down there by the ditch and get him out of the sun. Plenty of hay and water for him there, too."

"Noticed your fields. That all you grow—hay?"

"Just about. Making a living, such as it is, selling it to the army at Fort McDowell. Course I got a garden for truck. Can raise most anything in this ground long as you got water."

"Lot of work digging those ditches," Fontana commented, taking up the gelding's reins and starting for the designated shelter.

"Weren't me or none of the rest dug them. Was the Indians. All we done was clean them out. You aiming to head back to Lordsburg now that you see your friends ain't here?"

"Not much use. Think I'll go on to Tucson if there's a trail out of here."

"Better'n the one going to Lordsburg! Heads due south. Take you right to there—unless the 'Paches get in your way."

"They hostile?"

"Some of them are real unfriendly."

The lawman shrugged. "Well, friendly or not, I'll be leaving in the morning."

· 13 ·

There was no break in the heat, and by noon that next day John Fontana, well on the road to Tucson, a hundred miles or so ahead in the hazy, shimmering distance, found both himself and the sorrel suffering intensely. Still he pushed on, refusing to halt, taking only brief respite now and then in the filigree shade of mesquite and other sparse desert shrubs.

That he could wait for nightfall, do his traveling in the cooler hours, occurred to him but that would mean the loss of another day and this he would not consider.

He had taken the precaution of carrying extra water, now had a second canteen obtained from Cartwright. His stock of grub had also been replenished, partly from the small inventory carried by what served as a general store in Phoenix and partly from the larder of the hay farmer and his Papago squaw who, it turned out, was quite skilled in the preservation of food.

He would not want for sustenance, that was certain; but there were times, particularly on the second day out, when the lawman wondered if he would be able to withstand the furious attack of the desert environment. And then as before, he stolidly pulled his hat lower over his eyes to cut down the blinding glare, loosened more clothing and pressed on. He would survive. He must.

The useless ride to Phoenix had cost him the better part of a week and that knowledge was a bull-head burr pricking him incessantly. Four days to Phoenix, another two or so in reaching Tucson—almost a full week. If he had gone straight to the latter from Lordsburg, he would have already been there, completed his purpose, and moved on.

Of course there was no guarantee that any of the outlaws were in Tucson, but it was logical. Tallent and Glade had been on the road that came from the ancient Mexican settlement; and Nick Tallent, dying, had turned him away from that point. He was certain now the pair had been coming from

65

there, and just as sure their two partners had remained. The incident, however, had not been a total loss. There had been seven killers to reckon with; now there were only five.

One little, two little, three little Indians. . . . The rhyme rocked through his mind. As in the ditty, the number was beginning to decrease. Now there were only five, and if his luck held, soon there would be but three. He had accomplished that much.

Who would he find in Tucson? Would one of them be Bart? He hadn't given that eventual possibility much thought but now the words of the Lordsburg marshal, linked to similar comments others had made concerning such confrontation, began to pick at his mind. What if Bart chose to resist as had Bill Glade and Tallent? Could he draw and shoot him down—his own blood kin—as coolly as he had them?

Or would he hesitate a few costly seconds while he struggled with himself over the right or wrong of it, and give his brother an opportunity to escape or perhaps even rob him of his own life?

There'd been no uncertainty where Tallent and Glade were concerned, there'd be none when the showdown with Bart came. He was an outlaw, a killer, no different from the six others he ran with; he deserved no more or no less than they. Hadn't they gunned him just as they had driven bullets into the rest of the men who had been in the street beside him that day in Genesis?

Bart hadn't intervened for him, could even have held the gun that cut him down for all he knew. Why should he be disturbed over the possibility of returning the favor in kind? Bart had never been a brother in the true sense of the word, not since the days when they were small boys on the family farm, and those flaming moments in Genesis proved he had not changed.

No! The hell with Bart and blood ties and all that! He was the same as the others, a stranger, a killer, a cold-blooded murderer; he would be made to pay in one way or the other just as would his renegade friends.

Beat by the heat, eyes red and smarting from the glare, Fontana halted at dark in the low hills not far from where he figured Tucson would be found. He felt he should go on, not stop until he reached the settlement, but his flogged body would not agree.

And it could be dangerous. It was best he arrive there rested and in the best condition possible in the event he encountered the outlaws immediately and was called upon to use his gun. In his present state he'd be no match for them or anyone else only half skilled with a weapon—and they were experts.

Loosening the sorrel's saddle girth and slipping the bridle, he picketed the horse on a small splash of grass he found between two large boulders and sought out a place for himself. He'd not build a fire and prepare a meal just yet, not until it was sufficiently night and the smoke would go unnoticed.

He had not forgotten Cartwright's warning of hostile Apaches, and while there had been no sign of any during the passage so far, he was unwilling to take any risks. It would be a hell of a note to have come this far, accomplishing what he had, be on the threshold of accomplishing even more, only to have an Apache's bullet put an end to it all.

With darkness the heat decreased and Fontana began to feel alive once again. After giving the sorrel a good drink, he requisitioned even more from his depleted canteens and indulged in the luxury of a wet-rag rub down before busying himself at preparing a meal of coffee, fried meat, grease soaked bread, also fried, and a jar of the squaw's preserved peaches.

Feeling much improved, he was at the point of tightening the sorrel's saddle and continuing the journey when a faint sound at the mouth of the small canyon in which he had made camp, brought him around.

A brave, feathered lance in one hand, white band encircling his head, dabs of ochre streaking his dark face, sat astride a lean pony staring at him. In the pale moonlight the Apache looked unreal.

For a long breath the two locked glances, each equally startled by the other, and then Fontana's hand darted for the weapon on his hip. Instantly the brave thumped his heels against the flanks of his mount. The wiry little horse lunged forward, was gone behind a shoulder of rock that stood at the entrance to the box.

The lawman wheeled at once. There had been only one Apache—but there would be others nearby. It was best he not be there when the entire party returned. Gathering his gear, he stowed it in his saddlebags, hurriedly readied the sorrel, and mounting, rode out of the canyon.

He cut left, south in the direction he needed to go. Fortunately the Apache had been pointed north, had continued on that course. . . . Something had drawn him to the canyon for a look—the smell of smoke in the stilled air, or perhaps the faint glow of the fire, although small, on the rocks above. He would carry word of the lone white man to the rest of his party and all would move in quickly for the kill.

Walking the sorrel at a fast gait, Fontana moved away from his camp, slanting for a dark band of cedars and brush several hundred yards on ahead. If he could reach that cover before the braves returned his chances for shaking them were good. But he must use care; to spur the sorrel, break him into a gallop with its resulting drum of hoof beats, would be a certain giveaway. There was no choice but to move slowly and quietly, and to suppress the urge to take rapid flight.

He heard a yell just as he gained the cedars, knew at once that he had been spotted. Ducking into the shadows, he roweled the sorrel into a trot, endeavoring to keep the outer fringe of trees between himself and the Apaches. He could hear them coming up fast, the thud of their horses clear in the hush.

The gelding stumbled in the tangled growth, fell to a walk. There was no hope for haste and Fontana knew it was equally hopeless to attempt to outrun the braves in the open, with the horse as tired as he was. Suddenly angered at being trapped in such a predicament, blaming Nick Tallent again for bringing it about, he wheeled, cut through the cedars at right angles. He could only hope to hide, let the Apaches bypass him. . . . If that failed—

The hammer of the oncoming Indians grew louder, slowed. They were swinging off the open ground, entering the trees, undoubtedly suspecting he would attempt to hide. Abruptly the lawman halted in a dense clump of oak, searched the cedars on beyond for an indication of the Apaches' exact position. Faint motion directly opposite warned him. They were close, were now filtering softly through the growth in the hopes of flushing him out.

The faint swish of a branch only steps away stilled him. Tense, praying the sorrel would make no move or sound, he drew his pistol and waited out the dragging moments. The Apache would pass only a stride beyond. If he should glance to his left the deadly game of hide and seek would be over—with him the loser.

An irregular blur of white passed through an opening in

the brush before him. . . . One of the Indian ponies. The brave came into view. He was hunched forward, silhouetted face intent, dully shining body taut. Abruptly he was gone from sight, swallowed up by the brush. Fontana waited. There could be others following him. He rode out a long minute, two—three. He dare not hold back further; the Apaches could decide to double back in the belief they had overshot him.

Spurring the sorrel lightly, he pulled out of the oak clump, moving straight on for the edge of the trees. The Indians were now between him and Tucson but within the band of dense growth, and safety, if there was such a thing, lay past them.

He crossed the narrow strip, halted at its fringe. Slipping off the gelding, he hurried to a large rock, crawled to its summit, and threw his glance along the edge of the lengthy grove. No riders were in sight. The Apaches were still in the cedars.

Returning to the sorrel he swung onto the saddle, and keeping just within the band of green, rode slowly southward, taking care to neither break into the open nor drift too deep into the brush.

A guttural voice spoke into the night. Fontana halted instantly. The sound had come from behind and to his left. An answer, farther over and also in back of him followed. He grinned tightly. The Apaches were doing as he'd expected— back-tracking through the shadowy grove in the belief that he was still there.

He waited out a quarter hour and then rode on, still relying on the brush for cover but now urging the gelding to a faster pace than before. Miles later, with the horse lagging badly, he turned into another pocket in the rocks, this one much better screened then the first, and halted for the balance of the night.

Fontana was up before sunrise, and passing by the usual morning meal, pressed on for Tucson, already simmering in the heat when he reached there around mid-morning. He had gotten some rest and he felt good as he swung into the end of the settlement's main street and advanced slowly between the twin rows of buildings. . . . First he'd find a restaurant where he could get a meal, and maybe he'd treat himself to a couple of drinks. After that he'd be ready.

His eyes narrowed. He reined in the sorrel. A man, a

large, slope-shouldered individual with thick chest and long, powerful-looking arms bared to the sun, was crossing the street a short distance ahead. Grim satisfaction surged through the lawman. . . . Rufe Cobb.

· 14 ·

Silent, cool purpose flowing smoothly through him, John Fontana watched the outlaw cross over to a squat structure, above the door of which was the lettered sign CANTINA, and enter. His first impulse was to drop from the saddle, challenge Cobb, and have it out then and there, but caution stayed him; there would be another of the killers somewhere nearby, perhaps inside the saloon. Let Cobb lead the way to him.

Moving on, the lawman slanted in to the hitchrack at the side of the adobe brick building where a half dozen horses waited in hip-shot, tail-switching somnolence, and dismounted. Tying the sorrel, he checked the weapon on his hip, strode to the door, and stepped quickly inside. There was no wooden porch or landing to the saloon, only the hard-baked dirt of the street which permitted him to approach without sound.

Upon entering, Fontana edged to the side, out of the doorway's silhouetting frame, and stood motionless against the cool wall while his eyes adjusted to the change. It was a small place, lit only by deep-set windows on two sides and a few lamps suspended from a beam ceiling.

The bar was no more than a crudely constructed platform, narrow in width and eight or ten feet in length. There was no mirror behind it, simply a stair-step of shelves that supported a good stock of liquor. Chairs were scattered about the two or three tables.

He saw Cobb at one of those, and the anger within him began to pound. The outlaw's back was to him, and the man facing him from across the table was not one of the gang. Fontana's hopes sagged. Again he searched the faces of the remaining half dozen men in the room. All were strangers.

He continued to wait there in the shadow, aware of the bartender's attention, debating what course to follow—hold back, wait on the chance Cobb's partner would put in an

71

appearance, or make his play? The old saw pertaining to a bird in the hand being worth two in the bush trickled through his thoughts, brought him to a decision. He had no real assurance that the other outlaw was in Tucson; it had only been probable—and he'd not gamble on that.

Suddenly taut, a high-shouldered figure limping slightly, Fontana moved through the lazily drifting layers of smoke and pulled up an arm's length behind Cobb. The saloon had fallen silent.

"Cobb—I'm taking you in for murder."

The outlaw, hunched forward, elbows on the table, straightened, twisted about slowly. His eyes flared as he recognized Fontana, and then a sardonic smile cracked his lips.

"Well, if it ain't the kid brother!"

The lawman, struggling to control the hate and anger the mere sight of the outlaw evoked within him, drew back a step.

"Get up—goddamn you to hell!"

Rufe Cobb muttered something under his breath, and arms raised, came to his feet. The man opposite him, slim and narrow-faced, started to move. He froze as Fontana's harsh voice lashed out at him.

"Hold it! Stay where you are—hands flat on that table. Try something and you're dead." Without turning, he added to the others in the saloon. "Goes for all of you."

Cobb came fully around, a poised, hulking brute of a man who matched Fontana's towering size.

"What're you aiming to do?"

"Send you back to Santa Fe for hanging—or kill you trying—"

"Not me!" Cobb yelled and lunged forward.

The gun in the lawman's hand rapped sharply, filling the saloon with deafening echoes. The bullet thudded into the table's top and the man sitting obediently at it threw himself over backward, rolled frantically to get out of harm's way.

Fontana, off balance, caught at Cobb's arm, steadied himself, and lashed out with the heavy pistol. The barrel caught the outlaw on the side of the head, slashed a gash along the cheek with its sight. Cobb howled, struck out with both hamlike fists. The weapon, knocked from the lawman's grasp, fell to the floor, went skittering off into a nearby corner.

Cursing, Fontana grabbed at the outlaw, found good purchase for his fingers in the man's shirt. Rocking to the

side, he whirled Cobb half about, and now with rage a
seething flame burning within him, drove a solid right into
the man's jaw.

The outlaw staggered into the table, lowered both arms.
Fontana rushed in relentlessly, rock-hard knuckles pounding
the big man mercilessly. Cobb began to sink. The lawman
raised a booted foot, kicked him hard in the belly, stalling
him. At once he swung, smashed a jolting blow to the
temple, stepped away.

Any ordinary man would have dropped to his knees. Cobb
only groaned, and legs spread, arms hanging loosely, shook
himself. Fontana was breathing hard. His entire body was
protesting at the strain it was undergoing but he paid no
heed.

Crowding in, he aimed another shocking right at Cobb's
jaw. The outlaw jerked away, avoided it. He collided with
one of the chairs, kicked it into Fontana's legs. The lawman
buckled forward, stumbling against the heavily built piece
of furniture. In that moment of distraction Rufe Cobb swung.
His balled hand caught Fontana on the chin, drove him back.

Senses reeling, the lawman fought to keep from going
down. Through a faint mist he saw the outlaw, grinning
wickedly, circling the chair, big arms raised, huge fists
cocked. Fontana drew away shaking his head, trying to clear
it.

Cheers were going up in the saloon. Cobb rushed in, con-
fident of victory. Instinctively Fontana jumped aside. His
mind had cleared now and the weakness the outlaw's blow
had induced was swiftly fading. He pulled away again as
Cobb wheeled, came for him once more. Abruptly he
halted. Feet solidly planted, he brought up his left arm,
elbow stiff, held it rigidly extended.

The outlaw came into it at full stride. It rocked him
back to his heels, spun him half about. Fontana's right,
following an instant later, with all the strength he could mus-
ter, landed squarely on his cheek.

The crack of the bone was audible throughout the saloon.
Cobb yelled, went to one knee, caught at the table to save
himself from falling to the floor. The lawman surged in.
A low-traveling left to the opposite side of the outlaw's head
brought another yell of pain from him. He staggered upright, both hands held palms forward to Fontana as if beg-
ging the lawman to stop. His face had an odd, lopsided shape.

Heedless, Fontana closed in. He drove both fists into the

outlaw's middle, arms working like steam-driven pistons. Cobb began to wilt, his knees bowing slowly. The lawman seized him by the shirtfront, spun him about, slammed him backward onto the table, head and shoulders hanging over its edge.

"You're dead, damn you!" he raged. "Dead as all those people you killed!"

Cobb struggled to roll off the table, ease the strain on his arched backbone. Someone in the crowd voiced a protest but none had the courage to step forward, attempt to dissuade the big lawman.

"Your partner—where is he?" Fontana demanded, pressing down hard on the outlaw's throat with a hand, while pinning his legs with his body.

"Gone—don't know where—" Cob gasped.

"The hell you don't!" the lawman yelled. "There's one of that bunch here with you. Know that for sure. Who is it—Bart?"

"Was . . . Buck. . . . He's gone—"

"That's a lie!" Fontana shot back, bearing down harder.

"No—the truth—"

"For God's sake, mister," a voice called desperately from the crowd, "you're breaking his back—and he's telling you right if you're meaning that fellow that come here with him."

"Was two other'n," a second voice volunteered. "They lit out for El Paso, somebody said."

John Fontana, the fierce, soaring hate within him beginning to subside, straightened, relaxed the pressure of his weight on the outlaw.

"Know about them," he said in a low, grinding voice. "The one that stayed—Buckram—where'd he go?"

"Ain't sure. On west, or maybe it was south."

At once the lawman turned to Cobb. The outlaw groaned, tried to avoid the lawman's hands.

"Where is he? Tell me or—"

"Prieta!" Cobb fairly screamed the answer. "Went there to gamble!"

Again Fontana drew back. A frown creased his sweaty face. "Prieta," he repeated.

"Agua Prieta," someone at the bar explained. "Town on the border."

The lawman turned away, stepped to the corner of the room, and retrieved his weapon. Still holding it, he fixed the crowd with his bitter, thrusting glance.

"Anybody seen him there lately?"

"Reckon I have." A man dressed in a checked suit and obviously a drummer spoke up. "Leastwise if it's Tom Sweeney you're talking about. Was there a week ago. Didn't know it was him you meant."

Fontana crossed to where Cobb, moaning softly and with both hands clapped to his swollen face, leaned against the table.

"That what he's calling himself—Sweeney?"

The outlaw nodded carefully. His pistol was still in its holster, held there by a rawhide loop over the hammer. Releasing the weapon, the lawman slipped it under his belt, and pulling Cobb upright, he turned to the crowd.

"Where's the sheriff's office?"

"Down the street, to the right."

Fontana gave Cobb a push toward the door. "Move out," he said. "And don't try getting away. I'll kill you same as I did Glade and Tallent."

Rufe Cobb only groaned.

"Holding you to account for this prisoner," Fontana said a short time later as the elderly sheriff of Tucson locked the door of the cell into which he had placed the outlaw. "He gets away before the marshal comes for him, I'll be back to see you."

The lawman's lean face hardened. "Well, maybe you'd just better take him to Santa Fe yourself," he said stiffly, offering to return the warrant Fontana had given him.

Fontana shook his head. "Job's not finished—only about half. How long'll it take me to get to Agua Prieta?"

"Couple of days. Who you looking for there?"

"Name's Buckram. Been calling himself Sweeney around here."

The sheriff nodded. "Yeh, recollect him. Gambler." He paused, glanced at Cobb slumped on the cot in his cage and nursing his broken jaw. "Expect I'd best call the doc for him. . . . You sure must've hit him mighty hard."

Fontana gingerly touched the side of his own battered face. There was swelling there, too.

"Ought to figure himself lucky," he said, and turned for the doorway.

· 15 ·

Agua Prieta, a small, sun-parched settlement, lay sprawled on the indefinite line that separated Arizona and Mexico. It appeared deserted in the driving heat when John Fontana rode in late in the afternoon of his third day out of Tucson. He should have arrived much sooner but midway the sorrel began to go lame and he was forced to slacken the pace as well as halt numerous times, and thus lost almost a full day.

He veered into the first livery stable in sight, and turning the gelding over to the hostler with instructions as to his general care and attention to the leg the horse was favoring, he said, "You the owner?"

The hostler was middle-aged, had a tobacco-stained beard and several missing teeth. In the interest of coolness he wore no shirt under his bib overalls, leaving his arms and bony shoulders exposed.

"Reckon I am. Jubal Smith's the name."

"Know a gambler around here called Tom Sweeney?"

Smith cocked his head to one side. "Seen him a few times."

"Where can I find him?"

"Me not being his pa, I rightly wouldn't know," the liveryman drawled. "But was I looking for him I'd go to the Spur."

"The Spur?"

"Saloon down the street a piece. . . . You a friend of his'n?"

"Hardly," Fontana murmured, and moved out into the lowering sunlight.

He saw the sign designating the saloon when he started down the street. It appeared to be either half in each of the two countries or just on the American side of the border. With the commingling of persons, some in ordinary civilian attire, others in military uniforms, which was taking place in front of the building, it was difficult to tell.

Fontana strode purposefully on through the dust, the limp acquired at Genesis more pronounced now as always at the end of the day when weariness began to take its toll of him. But such had no part in his thoughts.

Buck Buckram. . . . A sort of relief had coursed through him when Rufe Cobb had revealed the name of his partner, and that was now disturbing him. Why relief? Was it because it was not Bart that he was soon to confront? It shouldn't make any difference—and it couldn't. He'd convinced himself of that fact earlier, yet there was no denying he had felt a lessening of tension.

He did not like the realization and it set up a vague worry within him, but minutes later he shook it from his mind as he halted at the corner of the structure housing the Spur and centered his attention on the business at hand.

The saloon was on the Arizona side, he saw, taking note of the area. Only a stride beyond lay the border, marked by a sagging wire fence that was down in many places. Evidently little attention was paid by either side to the boundary, and passage back and forth between the two countries and their adjacent settlements went unhampered and unnoticed.

Glancing about and seeing no familiar faces, Fontana stepped up onto the porch of the building and entered. The place was large and busy. Two dozen or more patrons were present despite the early hour, and the side room devoted to gambling of all sorts—chuck-a-luck, poker, blackjack, keno, even roulette—was crowded.

The lawman crossed to the long bar, ordered a whiskey, and hooking his elbows on the edge of the counter, gave the room close scrutiny over the rim of his glass. He found Buckram. The redhead was at a table in the back. Three other men were sitting in the game with him, and a small, dark-haired woman with pale skin and large doelike eyes stood at his shoulder.

A bleakness covered Fontana's features as he studied the outlaw, while within him the same hard core of pitiless anger that had gripped him on the two previous occasions of confrontation took possession. Buckram looked prosperous, contented, completely self-assured, as he played his cards, using the money he had so ruthlessly killed to obtain.

Suddenly unable to watch any longer, Fontana slammed his empty glass to the sawdust-covered floor, and dropping a hand to the pistol on his hip, shouldered his way through the crowd to where the outlaw sat.

As he halted, one of the players looked up indifferently, shook his head. "Game ain't open."

"Go to hell!" he snapped, and drawing his weapon jammed the barrel into the killer's back. "You're done, Buckram. . . . Get up—slow."

The outlaw stiffened as the other players pulled back hastily. From the corner of his eye Fontana saw the girl turn quickly, fear tearing at her face.

"Keep out of this—everybody!" the lawman warned, and dug the pistol deeper into the outlaw's back.

Buckram rose cautiously, twisting his head about. "What's this all—" he began, and then the words choked in his throat as he recognized Fontana.

"You're going to hang, Buck," the lawman said in a tight voice. "I'm sending you to Santa Fe and—"

"No!" the woman screamed and threw herself against Fontana.

The big man cursed, staggered to one side, badly off balance. Buckram spun, hurled the cards he was holding into the lawman's face, and lunged through the open doorway behind him.

Grim, unable to shoot because of the girl and the men stumbling to get out of his way, Fontana cleared a path with his hands and followed the outlaw into the open.

He had a quick glimpse of Buckram, on the Mexican side of the fence, ducking between two adobe huts. He snapped a shot at the fleeing man, saw dust spurt from one of the mud bricks beyond him. Voices were yelling at him from the rear of the saloon, from farther along the marker, and he could hear boots pounding on the dry, baked soil. He paid no heed, rushed on in pursuit of the outlaw.

Panting, sweat glistening on his face, he ran to the end of a short row of huts and broke out into a small plaza. The gambler was a hurrying figure on the opposite side.

"Buckram!" Fontana shouted.

The outlaw dodged instantly to one side, drew his weapon and fired.

The bullet was far wide. The lawman brought up his gun, hesitated as the outlaw darted into the open doorway of a closeby hut, knocking down an aged, brown man who had appeared. Immediately the lawman raced across the plaza, and hunched low, followed Buckram into the semi-dark of the small house. Two women, pulled back against the whitewashed wall, watched him enter with wooden expressions. At his pressing glance one pointed to the door of an adjoining room. Fontana hurried on, but with care. He was not anxious to blunder into an ambush.

Halting at the hut's rear entrance, he looked out into a narrow alleyway, saw no one, and stepped again into the open. It was a dead-end passage. Buckram could only have turned right. Immediately Fontana swung in that direction, ran to its end. The outlaw was a half-bent figure legging it for another alley two dozen yards away.

"Buck!" the lawman shouted once more as he raised his pistol.

The outlaw did not slow, but rushed on. Fontana steadied his weapon with his left hand, squeezed off a shot. Buckram paused in stride, twisted, and fell heavily.

Fontana, rage still burning bright within him, rodded the empties from his weapon, reloaded, aware of the pound of running feet, of shouts. Finished, he crossed slowly to where the outlaw lay. Hooking the toe of his boot under the man, he rolled him to his back. Buckram was dead.

"Four," the lawman murmured dully. "Leaves three."

"Senor—"

At the sharp call, Fontana turned. A half a dozen soldiers clad in the vivid blue uniform of the Mexican *Federales* faced him with leveled rifles.

"You will not move but to raise the hands!"

The lawman nodded, lifted his arms obediently. At once the *Federales* advanced, the young officer in command a step ahead.

"I've got a warrant for this man," Fontana said as the squad halted before him.

The Mexican stepped closer, drew the lawman's pistol from its holster and fell back. "Chavez—*mira!*" he barked.

One of the soldiers crossed to where Buckram lay, examined him briefly and returned to the line. "*Es muerto, teniente.*"

"You have killed this man."

Fontana's shoulders lifted slightly, fell. "He's an outlaw. Tracked him all the way from New Mexico. Can show you the warrant—"

"Do not try, senor!" the officer warned as the lawman started to reach for the packet of papers inside his shirt.

Fontana shook his head. Pearly Winnegar had prophesied

just such an incident, he recalled as he glanced about at the slowly gathering crowd of stolid, dry faces staring at him sullenly. He shifted his eyes to the Spur. A number of his countrymen were watching with interest but none were making an effort to be of help. Evidently when there was trouble all took pains to be definitely on the Arizona side of the line.

"You will come with me to Captain Rodriguez," the officer said briskly. "I warn you, do not try to escape. My men shoot well."

"Whatever you say, sergeant."

The Mexican's lips tightened. *"Teniente*—lieutenant," he corrected. "Lieutenant Ortega."

"All right, Lieutenant Ortega, let's go see your captain, get this over with."

• 16 •

It was cool inside the low, rambling structure in which the Mexican authorities maintained headquarters. The lawman was ushered into one of the forward rooms where a dark-eyed, swarthy man, resplendent in blue and much gold braid, was seated behind a desk. He listened attentively to the younger officer's report, rendered in a quick flow of Spanish, and then leaned back.

"Your name, senor?"

"John Fontana."

Rodriguez bridged his thin, tapered fingers. "So, John Fontana, it is a murder we have to deal with," he said in careful English.

The lawman shrugged. "If you can call shooting down a killer murder."

The officer's expression did not change. "Nevertheless, Lieutenant Ortega tells me you have entered my country and slain this man."

"He was an outlaw wanted by my government. I've got a warrant for him."

"Such papers are not good here—"

"You'd rather let a killer run loose, maybe make a lot of trouble for you, than permit a lawman to take him back where he'd be hung?"

"This one is dead. He cannot be taken back and punished, as you say."

"Way he wanted it. I tried to arrest him so he could be brought to trial."

Rodriguez nodded slowly. "I am to understand that you are a lawman?"

"Right," Fontana said, and drew the warrants from inside his shirt. Selecting the one covering Buckram, he handed it to the officer. "Here's the warrant I was talking about. Signed by the United States marshal and the governor of the territory."

81

Rodriguez read it painstakingly. "The name of this dead man is Buckram?"

"That's him. Was part of a gang that killed several people in a town where I was marshal. After they did their robbing and killing, they burned it to the ground. Left me for dead. Took me a month to get back on my feet. I've been trailing them ever since."

Ortega stepped forward, spoke quietly to his superior. Finished, he dropped back to his position behind Fontana. Outside the soldiers were talking among themselves in the quick, staccato manner of the Spanish language.

Rodriguez looked up, features intent. "I have been told a strange thing. Lieutenant Ortega tells me the dead man is known by the name of Sweeney. You speak of one called Buckram. Also, that is the name on your paper."

"They all changed their names," the lawman said impatiently. "Hell, wouldn't you if you'd been one of them?"

"It is not a question for me to answer. I am concerned only that you have entered my country, slain a man whose name is not the same as that written on your paper. Such creates a serious problem."

"Not far as I can see. I'll take the body if you want, haul it back across the border, and turn it over to the sheriff or whoever's in charge there. He'll certify that Buckram's dead on the warrant and send it back to Santa Fe. . . . That'll be the end of it."

Rodriguez gave that thought. "In words it is simple, in consequence it is not. You have other warrants."

"Three more. Had seven to start with."

"All but the three—it was necessary to kill them also?"

Fontana did not miss the implication. "Two of them put up a fight. They're dead. Other one's in jail at Tucson waiting for the marshal to come after him. They all get their chance to quit."

"Doubtless," Rodriguez said drily. "The three who yet remain, are they in Agua Prieta?"

"Was told they headed for El Paso. Figure to go there and see—soon as I leave here."

A large fly, trapped against the pane of a window, buzzed noisily. Lieutenant Ortega, standing firmly at attention, shifted uncomfortably.

"I fear such is impossible, senor," the captain said in his quiet, overly polite way. "You have broken a law of my country. It will be necessary to detain you until my superior arrives. He will decide what must be done."

Fontana stirred angrily. He could find himself penned up in a Mexican jail for weeks, even months, awaiting a decision of the military. Meanwhile word of the fate that had befallen Tallent, Glade, Rufe Cobb, and Buckram could catch up with the remaining members of the gang, send them into hiding.

"No reason for it," he said heavily. "I came here on law business. Got a signed warrant. Buckram just happened to pick your side of the border to make a try at running from me. Been no harm done far as you're concerned."

"Only that you *Norte Americanos* appear to believe you can do such at your pleasure. Our countries have a treaty. You do not honor it. . . . Had you come first to me with your warrant—"

"How the hell could I?" Fontana snapped. "When I found Buckram he was in that saloon on the Arizona side. He got away from me, ducked across the line."

"If such is true it would have been better had you not followed but come to me then. Many of our citizens were endangered by your shooting."

The lawman swore. They were going around and around, getting nowhere, but the possibility of being thrown into a cell for an indefinite length of time was a future he didn't relish.

"There somebody on the American side I can get to vouch for me, help straighten this out?"

The captain shrugged. His dark features glistened with a layer of sweat, and reaching up he smoothed the neatly clipped mustache that graced his upper lip.

"There is no one, senor. This is a matter of the Mexican government," he replied, and raised his dark eyes to the junior officer. *"Teniente,* this man will be locked in a cell to await the arrival of Colonel Valdez. You will see to such."

Ortega, snapping to attention, stepped up, seized Fontana by the arm. The lawman shook him off angrily, and suddenly reaching forward, snatched the warrant covering Buckram from the *Federale's* desk.

"I'm keeping this," he snarled.

In that same moment of confusion he wheeled, drove his shoulder into the slightly built Ortega, and jerked the pistol that had been taken from him from the young officer's belt. Circling the desk in two strides, he pressed the barrel of the weapon against Rodriguez' head.

"I'm going back across the border, Ortega," he said quietly as the lieutenant recovered his balance and took a quick step forward. "Your captain's going to be my escort. You or anybody else tries to stop me, he's dead. Understand?"

Ortega, seething with anger, spat out a stream of rapid Spanish. Rodriguez shook his head. "He understands, but I cannot guarantee my other men. They will wonder—"

"Tell the lieutenant to warn them. . . . Let's go."

The officer relayed the order, got slowly to his feet. Fontana plucked the pistol from its flapped holster at his side, tossed it into a far corner of the room.

"Now, march," he ordered, prodding the older man roughly toward the door. "You've got me tagged a killer. Keep believing it and you'll stay alive."

Glowering, Ortega stepped in front of them to lead the way. Several soldiers glanced up as they moved into the open and turned left for the ruptured fence that marked the boundary. The lieutenant said something in reply to their unspoken question, continued.

Tension settled over John Fontana, gripped him tight, sent a fresh flood of perspiration oozing from his body. His back was now to the *Federale* soldiers. Any one of them could swing up his rifle and put a bullet into him. Only his promise to kill Rodriguez should there be any interference was keeping him alive.

They reached the corner of the next building, rounded it. The border lay before them, no more than ten yards distant.

"You're doing fine, *amigos*," the lawman murmured.

They came to the section where the fence had been removed entirely. Two Mexican guards drew to attention when they saw the approaching officers, frowned as their glances shifted to Fontana, walking close behind the older man with pistol pressed into his spine. Again Ortega spoke, shook his head.

On the American side only casual notice was being taken. Two cowhands, squatted on their heels in a discussion of some sort, glanced up briefly, resumed their conversation. Several soldiers in faded cavalry garb gathered around a buggy in which there were two young and pretty girls, failed to even look, while the few other men moving about in front of the Spur continued about their business.

"Ortego—pull up," Fontana called quietly. "Far as you go. Turn around and head back."

The lieutenant wheeled, his features taut. "But my captain—"

"Nothing's going to happen to him long as he does what he's told. Aim to let him walk with me until I get to the other side of the saloon. Just doing a little guaranteeing myself."

"Go quickly," Rodriguez said in a strained voice. "And do nothing—*comprende?*"

"*Comprendo, mi capitan,*" the younger man answered. Pivoting stiffly, he retraced his path to the border.

"Not far now," the lawman said then to the *Federale*. We get to that next corner, turn it. Be leaving you there."

One of the soldiers had come about, was now glancing toward them, a frown on his face. Fontana ignored him, crowded closer to Rodriguez as he endeavored to hide the weapon he held against the officer. Two men came out of the saloon, passed on by without noticing.

They reached the end of the building. The Mexican obediently rounded the corner, halted. At once the lawman pushed by.

"Don't like to have treated you this way, Captain," he said, holstering his pistol, "but I sure couldn't waste a lot of time laying out in your jail. *Adios.*"

"For not long, my friend," the officer said with a bland smile.

Fontana barely heard the softly spoken words as he hurried off, pointing for the livery stable up the street where he had left the sorrel. But the meaning of Rodriguez' veiled promise was not lost to him, only strengthened his desire to get as far from Agua Prieta as fast as possible before more trouble developed—and that could be a problem with a lame horse.

He came to the stable, hurried into its runway. Jubal Smith was dozing in a chair tipped against the wall.

"My sorrel," Fontana said, shaking the man roughly. "He ready to go?"

The stableman grinned toothlessly, wagged his head. "Mister, you ain't going nowheres on that horse—not for a spell anyways."

The lawman threw a glance toward the border. Rodriguez was speaking with Ortega and the two guards. He cut back to Smith.

"You saying he's too lame to ride?"

"Sure is. Be a week—ten days—"

"Can't wait that long. Got a horse I can buy?"

The stableman got to his feet. "Yeh, reckon I have. There's a good little black—four-year-old. He's—"

"Let's see him."

Smith turned, shambled off toward the rear of the stable, ragged overalls making a dry, rustling sound as he moved. Halting at the back door he pointed to a gelding in one corner of a corral.

"That there's the one."

The horse didn't look too bad, a bit lean but his legs appeared straight and strong. He should last to the next town—possibly all the way to El Paso.

"How much?"

Jubal scratched at his jaw. "Well, can't hardly part with him for less'n fifty dollars."

"I'll give you twenty-five and the sorrel. Take it or forget it."

The stableowner sighed. "All right, I'll take it."

Fontana dug into his pocket for the necessary funds, paid them over to the man. "Throw my gear on him quick—and get me a bill of sale. . . . Be right back."

Coming about, he hurried to the front of the stable, once more glanced down the street. The *Federale* captain and his lieutenant were no longer to be seen. Both had evidently returned to quarters—or had they? He wondered, recalling the final words spoken by Rodriguez. They had to mean something.

Suddenly convinced of it, Fontana turned, trotted back to the corral. Smith had the bridle installed on the black, was just heaving the saddle into place, his movents deliberate and unhurried. The lawman brushed him aside, fell to securing the tack. The cinch tight and tested, he swung onto the horse, spurred toward the gate.

"What about your bill of sale?" Jubal shouted, leaping back.

"Can't wait!" Fontana answered. "You try telling somebody I stole this black, I'll say you stole my sorrel!"

Hunched on the gelding, the lawman swept into the open, hesitated briefly to get his bearings, and swerved hard right—east. El Paso would lie somewhere in that direction.

At that moment he heard a shout, looked back. A man wearing a star was coming from the rear of the livery stable. Ortega was at his side. The *Federales* had called in the law to help them recover their escaped prisoner. Fontana grinned tightly. They'd have to ride like hell to catch him.

· 17 ·

They were going to try.

Such became evident to John Fontana a half hour later when the distinct drum of hoofbeats on his back trail reached him. Leaving Agua Prieta, he had ridden directly toward the range of mountains sprawling somewhat northeast, hoping to confuse any pursuers; later, in the interest of easier traveling, he had cut back to the border, where the land was of a more gentle conformation. The ruse had cost him time, looked now to have gone for naught.

But he would concede no more. By riding due east and maintaining a parallel course to the occasional mounds of rock that marked the border between the two countries, he figured he would eventually end up in El Paso, since, like Agua Prieta, it lay on the line. To vary his course now would take him away from his intended destination, and he was unwilling to lose any more time.

Glancing over his shoulder he saw the small roll of dust lifted by the riders coming in his wake—noticed also a similar but larger cloud farther south. It brought a grin to Fontana's heat-cracked lips. Evidently it was a dual operation; lawmen following on the Arizona side, *Federales* on the Mexican. He was to be given no opportunity to duck across the border at some convenient point and escape.

Brushing at the sweat on his bearded face, he gauged the sun; still several hours until full darkness. No help there. He would simply have to keep moving, stay ahead of them until night finally came. It shouldn't be too hard to throw them off his trail after that.

Roweling the black lightly, he increased his pace. The gelding responded fairly well but his speed and stamina were far below that which the sorrel would have exhibited. However, they were crossing a broad expanse of sand and the loose footing could be the cause.

Such was only partly true. A time later he saw that he was losing the race; the two men on his trail had gained ground and the dust cloud kicked up by the Mexicans was also nearer.

The black just didn't have it. Had it been the sorrel under him he would by now have widened the gap. Raising his glance he looked ahead. A mile or so in the distance a jutting rock offered possibilities. If he could reach its yonder side well before his pursuers, he might be able to pull into a draw or some such screening object, permit them to override him as the Apaches had done. He could then lie low until darkness.

It was his only choice unless he wished to halt, make a stand, and possibly go to gunplay with the two riders, undoubtedly a sheriff and his deputy—and he had no desire to do that. Once more spurring the rapidly tiring black, he began to veer toward the rocks.

He reached the barren, heat-cracked formation and swung in behind it, slanting for a fair-sized arroyo overgrown with mesquite and plume. The black was heaving badly from the punishing run across the sand flat, and had the rocks been a mile farther, it was doubtful he could have made it. But the weary horse could rest now.

Most likely his change of course had been noted, but whether or not this was so, the lawmen would have no difficulty in following the gelding's tracks. He'd hoped for better cover beyond the pile of granite but there were only more plains sloping down from the mountains well to the north—and they were hopelessly out of the question. Turning his attention from them, Fontana shrugged resignedly. The black wasn't much of a horse. He'd do well to make it to El Paso.

Leaving the animal tied in the scanty shade, the lawman dropped back to the monolith and climbed to its crest. Spotting a pocket near its forward point he moved toward it. The surface of the rocks was still scalding hot from the heat stored up during the long day, and several times when he was forced to extend his arms and brace himself, he burned his hands.

Finally he was settled, crouched below the rim of the shallow bowl, and in a position to look down upon the riders when they rounded the formation in search of him. Just what he would do then, he was leaving to the moment itself when it faced him.

He did not have long to wait in the sweltering, breathless heat. Within only minutes he heard the steady thump of hoofs in the sand, and then shortly the two men rode into view. Raising his glance, Fontana noted that the *Federales* had also changed directions, now were pointed due north. He counted eight in the squad, but they presented no threat as long as he remained on the American side of the border. He shifted his attention back to the lawmen.

One was elderly, had thick white hair bushing out from under his wide-brimmed hat. He wore Confederate gray pants, white shirt, and a nondescript vest. A yellow bandana had been turned about and covered the lower part of his face, like a mask, to ward off the dust.

His companion was much younger. He was flashily dressed, with many silver conchos decorating his gear, and he sported two pistols, both pearl-handled. Undoubtedly he was quite impressive as he stalked about the streets of Agua Prieta.

Fontana watched them round the formation of rocks, halt. The older man pointed toward the arroyo in which the black waited, an indication to the lawman that they had spotted his horse, would guess him to be closeby. At such moments it was his belief that the advantage lay with the man who made the first move, and drawing his gun, he rose to his full height.

"Right here," he drawled.

The two lawmen, now proceeding with more caution, jerked to a startled stop. The younger man's hands dropped to his sides, his friend growled something in a hurried, warning tone, then forgot whatever he had in mind, allowed his arms to simply hang. The elderly lawman then settled back in his saddle and stared up at Fontana. With the bandana pulled clear he looked sharp-faced, almost wizened.

"Name's Jordan, sheriff of this county. This here's my deputy, Bill Yeager. You're Fontana, lawman from up New Mexico way, I'm told."

"Right,"

"Reckon you know what I've got to do—"

"Never was much good reading minds," Fontana said coolly.

"Have to take you back, turn you over to the Mexican authorities," Jordan said in a calm, dispassionate way. "You got yourself in a peck of trouble doing what you done."

Fontana shook his head. "Wasting your time, Sheriff. Nobody takes me back."

"Like as not they'll turn you loose after a spell," Jordan continued as if not hearing. "Just that they have to sort of keep up appearances. Can't let no American go running around over there shooting down—"

"Explained all that to Rodriguez. Buckram was an out-law—a killer."

"Ain't saying he wasn't, only it would've been better to've come to me in the first place. Man was in my bailiwick and it's my place to handle an outlaw."

"Not where I'm concerned. Running down the men I'm carrying warrants for is my job—mine alone. Intend to keep it that way."

Jordan considered Fontana's set features thoughtfully, finally nodded. "Reckon I can see your point, but it don't cut no hay with me. Have to look at things different down here on the border. I got to get along with them *Federales,* and doing that's my job same as keeping the peace."

"Don't look to me for help. The last three of that bunch I'm after's in El Paso. Not quitting until I've taken care of them—and nobody's stopping me."

Bill Yeager muttered under his breath, shifted angrily on his saddle. Fontana smiled thinly. "Don't get any ideas, Deputy. Never gunned down a man wearing a badge yet. Sure would hate to start with you."

Yeager glanced at Jordan. The older man's hunched shoulders stirred slightly. "Kind of funny talk coming from a lawman."

"No funnier than you wanting to turn me over to the Mexicans when I was only doing my job."

"Could've held off until Sweeney come back across the line," Jordan insisted petulantly, "or you could've looked me up, let me talk to Rodriguez. . . . This here busting right in, taking it on yourself—"

"Not much of a hand to shove my chores off on somebody else. Always have believed in skinning my own snakes."

"And I reckon you'd as soon kill a man if he got in your way while you was doing it."

"Just how it is. No point trying to explain what it's all about, but it started with me, and it's me that's going to finish it. Now, if you've got it all straight, the two of you best turn your horses around and head back to town. I'm through talking."

"You ain't willing to even go see Rodriguez, patch things up—"

"Think I've already made that plain."

"Yeh, reckon you have. And holding that gun makes it plainer. Let's go, Bill."

"One thing more," Fontana warned, "don't try trailing me. I'll be watching."

Jordan nodded glumly, and clucking to his horse, wheeled about. Bill Yeager swung in beside him, young face dark and angry.

"By God, was me, I'd—"

"You'd be dead before your time," the old lawman said in a gusty voice. "Just keep riding."

John Fontana remained on the rocks until the pair were lost to sight in the lowering glare, and then returned to the black. The gelding was rested, seemed fit to travel, but it was evident he had little stamina. What with being aboard a slow horse and keeping a sharp eye on his back trail, the ride to El Paso was going to be a long one, the lawman thought morosely as he swung onto the saddle.

• 18 •

"This here's Las Cruces, mister. You lost or something?"

Fontana stared down at the boy in patched shirt and made-over pants standing barefoot in the loose dust.

"Seems," he murmured. "Was headed for El Paso."

"It's that away," the youngster said, pointing off into the south. "Takes about a day, riding."

The lawman shrugged wearily. "Much obliged," he said, and glanced about. Las Cruces was a dozen small houses, a hotel, a few stores, and a fairly large building that bore the sign SALOON—CANTINA, as if the proprietor wished to be certain he would draw patronage from both Americans and Mexicans.

Somewhere back along the line he'd gotten off onto the wrong trail, ended up not at the border settlement of El Paso but miles to the north. Just where he slipped up he could not be sure; likely it was where there had been a sharp turn in the sporadic line of rock mounds, after which he had lost contact with them entirely.

It was going to cost a day and that didn't set well with him. He wanted to reach El Paso as soon as possible, settle with the remaining outlaws—Bart, Wayne Vetch, and Shorty Reece, and have done with it. Now it would have to wait. He swore, disgusted with himself, and touching the black with his spurs, crossed the street to the livery stable he saw there.

Leaving the gelding, he slung his saddlebags over a shoulder and stepped back into the afternoon sunlight. As well spend the night, take it easy; the rest would do both him and the horse good.

He went first to the hotel, the Amador, he noted as he entered. Signing the register, he went to his assigned room on the second floor, and stripping off sprawled on the bed. An hour later he rose, shaved, washed himself down from the bowl and pitcher provided, and donning a clean shirt, returned to the street. At least his appearance was somewhat improved, he reckoned, despite the faint discolorations still visible on his face—souvenirs of the fight with Rufe Cobb.

The sun was hovering near the crest of the mountains to the west, and feeling the need for a drink, he crossed to the saloon and entered. A half a dozen customers were lined up at the bar, and all of them turned to stare curiously at him. In no mood for either company or conversation, the lawman moved past them and settled at one of the tables.

The bartender came to him at once without being summoned, bringing a glass and a bottle. Keen interest highlighted his ruddy features.

"Whiskey?" he asked.

Fontana nodded brusquely. He guessed he shouldn't have taken those few minutes to doze; he felt worn, out of sorts.

The saloonman filled the glass and set it before him, bustling about like a hen with a solitary chick as he wiped the table with the tail of his apron, rearranged the other chairs, dusted the bottle, all during which he scarcely removed his eyes from the lawman's face.

After a bit Fontana reached out, wrapped his long fingers about the man's wrist. "Something about me bothering you?"

The bartender jerked away quickly. "No—no, sir. Just tidying up a bit so's things'll be clean for you."

"You got me figured for somebody special?"

"Well, no—or yes, I reckon so. You're the fellow that was over in Lordsburg a while back. Got in a ruckus with some big jasper and busted his jaw."

"How'd you know about that?"

"Was a whiskey drummer through here, told me. Said it was the dangdest fight he'd ever seen. . . . Knowed it had to be you, seeing that scar—"

The bartender's words broke off abruptly. An expression of fear and embarrassment spread over his features. "I—I didn't aim to say—"

"Forget it," the lawman said indifferently. "Mark's there. Nothing I can do about it."

"No, sir, sure can't. . . . Wish't I could've seen that fight. Must've been a real humdinger! Mind telling me what it was all about?"

"Personal business," Fontana said gruffly, and took up his glass. "Leave the bottle."

The saloonman bobbed, pushed the half-empty quart of whiskey to the center of the table, and hurried back to the counter and his waiting customers. At once he leaned forward, began to talk in a low-pitched, excited manner.

Fontana tossed off his drink, refilled the glass. The liquor was warm, bit deep, and shortly he began to feel its effects. He glanced toward the bar. The ruddy-faced saloonman was still talking, features bright and intent. No doubt he was recounting the whiskey drummer's report word by word, perhaps embellishing it with a few of his own.

The lawman stirred, shook his head. He wished to hell the drummer had kept his mouth shut. A tale such as he was spreading never did a man any good, served only to create trouble. There was always some ambitious handy-andy around wanting to test himself, see if he was as good, or hopefully, better. A reputation was something any sensible man didn't need if he wanted to live in peace.

Refilling his shot glass again Fontana stared moodily through the doorway into the dusty, deserted street. One thing good, he'd seen no more of Sheriff Jordan and his eager deputy, Bill Yeager. He'd convinced them to get off his back, let him go about his business, it would seem.

Three to go. . . . Methodically he ticked off their names in his mind—Reece, Vetch, Bart. It was narrowing down. Each time before, the odds had been longer where the possibility of confronting his brother was concerned. It was different now. Bart was one of the three remaining, and if all were together in El Paso, the showdown was at hand.

What would be the result? A month ago, even as near as two weeks ago, he would have been dead certain as to the outcome when the moment wherein he called upon Bart to surrender presented itself. Bart would submit or he would kill him; it had been that simple—that black and white. That, too, had changed.

Unwillingly, he was thinking about it again and that small thread of doubt was also again evident. Could he actually kill his own brother, his own flesh and blood? Why not? Bart was an outlaw, a heartless, cold, ruthless murderer the same as the others; why should he be considered as different?

He had no choice. His brother was no better, no worse than Shorty Reece, Tallent—all the others—and therefore could not be accorded any special treatment. As they must, he too must throw down his guns and prepare to answer to the law, or die. It was Bart's choice. He could make it easy on both of them or he could fight.

And that's where the rub would come. If Bart drew on him, Fontana knew he would have to protect himself; it was his duty as a lawman as well as his right. But would the fact that he was facing his own brother affect his thought process, bring about ever so brief a delay in his reflexes and slow his hand?

He must not permit it, not that he stood in fear of death, for the end came to everyone eventually, and a man could as well go out in a blaze of gunfire as lying flat on his back in bed. In the sort of life he'd led, and the calling he now followed, hell or heaven was always but a step away.

It was a knowledge you learned quickly to live with, a grim factor that governed your being, channeled your dreams, and constantly altered your plans. It made of you a solitary man, a loner, one reluctant to give of yourself to a woman and hope for a little in return from her. After all, what did you have to offer? Worry, fear, and, finally grief, and that was no gift—only a cross to be borne.

Fontana brimmed his glass, downed the whiskey impatiently. What the hell was the matter with him—mooning over something he could not change, pitying himself for his role in life—stewing about something that possibly would never come to pass. Always before, he'd taken things as they came, met and handled them. It would be the same when he stood face to face with Bart.

Forget it—forget it all! Have another drink, go hunt up the town's best restaurant, order a good meal, enjoy it, and then crawl into bed for a night's sleep. By morning he'd feel better—different.

"So you're the ring-tail cousin jack they're doing all the talking about!"

John Fontana did not turn his head, simply continued to stare woodenly into the street. . . . It had to come. He'd known that from the moment the bartender had started his yakking. . . . Goddam that whiskey peddler to hell, anyway!

• 19 •

"You hear me?"

Fontana eased back in his chair, looked up at the hulking man standing beside the table. Big, thick-shouldered and bull-necked, he had a round, heavy-jowled face, thick lips, and a nose that had been flattened thoroughly in some previous altercation.

"Sam's telling us you're a real stem-winding sonofabitch."

The lawman stiffened, considered the leering features of the man coldly. "You've got a mouth that's going to get you in trouble, mister."

"Name's Beaver, Jud Beaver—Mister Jud Beaver to you."

The bleak, lonely minutes at the table had done nothing to improve Fontana's mood. "Move on, Beaver. Go on home to your mama before you get in trouble."

The big man drew up angrily. His jaw hardened and a gleam came into his eyes. "Ain't nobody talks to me like that!"

"I am," the lawman said quietly, and filled his glass. "Now, let me be," he finished, and raised the liquor to his lips.

"Just like I figured, a four-flusher!" Beaver shouted, and lashing out with his thick arm, slapped the glass from Fontana's fingers.

Grinning broadly, Jud stepped back a step, shoulders hunched, balled fists hanging at his sides.

"Alway been looking to try my luck with a rip-snorter like you, see if they're as good as folks claim they are."

The hush that had fallen over the saloon was absolute. After a few moments, Sam, the bartender, spoke. His voice was anxious.

"Pull in your horns, Jud. He ain't bothering you and there's no sense starting something."

"There sure is," Beaver replied in a joyous sort of way. "Got a hunch that there yarn the drummer told you was nothing but a lot of bull!"

Fontana, wiping away the liquor splashed onto his face

96

with the back of a hand, studied the man silently while he clung tightly to his temper. He had troubles enough without this—something that was utterly senseless and for no good purpose. Beaver simply wanted to brawl, wanted to test himself against a man he'd heard was tough. There was no point in risking personal injury just to satisfy him.

"Better listen to your friend," he murmured.

Taking up the bottle he filled his glass once more, started to raise it. Still grinning, Jud Beaver stepped forward, arm extended. Patience exploded within John Fontana and he reacted swiftly. Knocking aside the big man's out-thrust hand, he threw the whiskey straight into his grimacing face, and starting a right fist from the floor, surged to his feet and drove it into Beaver's prominent belly.

Jud's wind burst from his flared lips in a raspy gust. He staggered back, both hands clutched to his middle, tripped over his own feet and sat down heavily.

The men at the bar laughed. Fontana, ignoring it, sank back into his chair, reached for the bottle again. A yell brought him to attention. He looked up. Jud Beaver, on his feet, had snatched up a chair, was hurling it at him.

Fontana ducked hastily. The chair sailed past him, crashed into the wall beyond. He lunged upright, anger gripping him as he braced to meet Jud Beaver's rush. He'd tried to avoid trouble, failed, and it was not in his makeup to back off.

He stepped quickly aside as the big man rushed in, caught him by the shoulder, stalled him, smashed a solid right to the jaw. Beaver cursed, and barely staggered by the blow, lashed out with clublike fists. The lawman took both in the body, winced at their driving force, and pulled away. Jud was after him instantly, crowding in close.

Fontana grunted as the man smashed him again in the ribs, sought to slow the attack with a stiff left to the face. This was no ordinary brawler he was up against, he realized; Beaver was strong and fast, had the kick of a mule in his fists and an amazing ability to absorb punishment.

He ducked as Jud swung a long, looping right at his head, countered with a solid smash to the man's jaw. Beaver blinked, grinned, continued to bore in. The lawman, beginning to strain for wind, stalled him once more with a stiff-elbowed left, tried for the ear with a hard right, missed.

The patrons of the saloon had pulled in closer, forming a half circle. They were yelling, voicing encouragement, some for Jud Beaver, others for Fontana. Sam, the bartender, was watching anxiously as the chairs and tables that kept getting in the way of the two big men were being reduced to splinters.

"You ain't so goddamn tough," Beaver rumbled between gasps for breath. "Reckon I could break your backbone like you tried doing that—"

Fontana blocked the words with a left to Beaver's mouth, a whistling right to his already flattened nose. The big man howled as blood blossomed on his lips and began to trickle down his chin. He spat, rid himself of two broken teeth.

Sweat soaking him, the lawman lashed out again, one fist driving solidly into Jud's face, the other into the side of the man's head. Beaver fell back a step, doubt and uncertainty showing on his battered features for the first time.

He half turned as if to pull away, pivoted suddenly, caught Fontana across the eyes. He tried to follow through with a blow to the jaw, missed as the lawman rocked, stumbled forward off balance. Fontana was upon him with the deadly quickness of a cat. He nailed Beaver with a short uppercut that snapped his head back, came down with a sledging right to the ear that drove the big man to his knees.

A cheer lifted from the crowd, more than doubled now by new arrivals attracted by the sounds of the conflict and forsaking whatever they were doing in the street.

Fontana waited, legs spread, left hand cupping the knuckles of his right where the skin had been scraped raw during the fight. Jud Beaver, down on his knees and supporting himself with stiffened arms, shook his head groggily.

"You satisfied?" the lawman asked tautly.

Beaver made no reply. After a time Fontana's shoulders relaxed and, shrugging, he turned away. Moving off a few steps, he picked up his hat, drew it on. If he—

"Look out!" a voice yelled in warning.

The lawman instinctively buckled, pivoted. His hand swept down for the pistol on his hip, came up. Jud Beaver, shamming before, was on his feet, gun leveled. The blast of the two weapons blended into a single, shocking report. Fontana felt the pluck of a bullet at his sleeve, heeled back the hammer of his weapon for a second shot. There was no need. Jud Beaver, head slung forward, arms dangling loosely, was slowly sinking to the floor.

Motionless, frustration and a heaviness settling over him, John Fontana watched through the layers of smoke drifting lazily before him. . . . Another man dead at his hand—and for no good reason. Where the outlaws were concerned he had no compunction, no regrets, but this man, this Jud Beaver, was only a waste.

Several of the men in the crowd pushed forward, doing so almost timidly. The lawman punched out the spent cartridge in the cylinder of his weapon, replaced it from the dully glinting row of brass that filled his belt.

"Dead, sure enough. . . . Right through the heart."

The words were spoken quietly as if the presence of death required hush.

"Had it coming to him," another voice said. "Was about to shoot that fellow in the back."

"I know—but killing—"

Fontana holstered his gun, turned away wearily. What the hell did they expect? A bullet killed, and in such critical moments a man had no time in which to pick his spot and try only to wound; he fired with but one thought in mind—keep from being killed. For all too many onlookers such incidents were as a game, to be won by the better man, and enjoyable in the watching, and then when it was over they were appalled by the outcome.

"Here's the marshal—"

Fontana leaned over, righted his table. The bottle of liquor lay on its side, had run out onto the floor, now had hardly a swallow left in it. He picked it up, glanced about for the glass.

"What's been going on here?"

"That's Jud Beaver laying there. Tried to shoot that fellow in the back, come out second best."

"The way it was, Tom. We all seen it."

Fontana turned his attention to the lawman. His eyes narrowed. Standing beside him was Jordan's deputy, Bill Yeager.

• 20 •

Yeager appeared tired and dusty. Evidently he had held back for a time and then, with or without Jordan's approval, had set out to follow him. Aware that El Paso was his intended destination, he had not taken the wrong turn but gone straight to the border settlement. Not finding his intended prisoner there he had guessed what had occurred and hurried north to Las Cruces.

The marshal stepped to where Beaver lay, considered him briefly. "Had it coming, I reckon," he said, and looked then at Fontana. He was a middle-aged man, squat, dark-faced, and wore a thick black mustache curving down over his mouth. "I'm Tom Locke. Reckon you can see I'm the marshal."

Fontana nodded. "Sorry about what's happened. Tried to—"

"He the man?" the marshal cut in, glancing at Yeager.

"That's him," Yeager replied firmly. "Name's Fontana. Claims he's a lawman."

"You for certain he ain't?"

Yeager's face flushed. "Don't see as it makes no difference. The Mexican government wants him. Up to me and Jordan to see they get him."

"Up to you maybe," Locke said drily, and then turned to Fontana. "What the deputy tells me about you true?"

Fontana leaned against the table, met the lawman's gaze coolly. "Depends on what he's told you."

"Claims you was in his town, Agua Prieta, and that you jumped the border and killed a man. Then when the *Federales* was taking you to jail you grabbed a gun and made the *Commandante* side you across the line."

"About the way of it, but not the whole thing. Man I shot was an outlaw—a killer. Got away from me in a saloon on the Arizona side, made a run for it. I went after him. He tried to gun me down, I beat him to it. Happened to be on Mexican ground."

The marshal digested that slowly. Then, "What about that

100

Commandante? You hold iron on him, make him take you back over?"

"Only way I could get past his soldiers."

Several in the crowd laughed, amused by the idea. Yeager bristled angrily.

"Ain't nothing funny about that! We've got an agreement with the Mexican guv'ment. Up to me and Jordan to see that it's lived up to."

"They ain't so set on keeping their *bandidos* from raiding on our side," someone pointed out.

Locke waited for the quick clamor of agreement to subside. Brushing at his mustache, he faced Fontana. "This a personal war of yours or are you a lawman?"

"I am," he said, ignoring the first part of the question. "Was a marshal in a town over in the western part of the territory. Man I was after, and six others, rode in one day. Killed several people, took all the cash they could find, and burned the place to the ground. Nothing left now."

"And you're out tracking them down—"

"What I'm doing. Carry warrants for them all, signed by the U.S. marshal and the governor."

"You got them handy?"

The lawman opened his shirt, retrieved the billfold, and handed the papers to Locke, who thumbed through them idly.

"Only four here. That mean you've caught up with three of them?"

"Four. One with the name Buckram on it—he's the man we're talking about. Never got the chance to turn it over to the sheriff."

The lawman refolded the warrants, passed them back to Fontana, who restored them to their case. "Don't see nothing wrong here," he said to Yeager.

The young deputy swore hotly. "There's a plenty wrong! He broke the law—the guv'ment law going over into Mexico after that man and killing him!"

"Seems to me he done them Mexicans a favor," a man somewhere in the crowd observed.

"Not the point!" Yeager insisted. "A man can't just run across the line and do something like that. There's rules and regulations. Got to be done proper like."

"Now and then there ain't time to follow the rules," Locke said patiently. "After you've wore that star for a spell, you'll know that."

"All I know," the deputy said stubbornly, "is I got to take this man back and hand him over to the *Federales.*"

Fontana stirred tiredly. He was feeling the aftereffects of Jud Beaver's smashing blows, and it had been a long day. As well bring the argument to a head, find out where he stood.

"You bring a warrant—one that'll be good in New Mexico?" he asked.

"Well, no. Didn't have time—"

"Then you're doing a lot of jawing for nothing. I'm not going back with you, for sure, and I don't figure you're big enough to take me, so unless the marshal here aims to side in with you, best you forget it."

Yeager turned to Tom Locke. "You going to arrest him, turn him over to me? You sort've owe it to Jordan."

The marshal gave that thought, shrugged. "Reckon I do owe Ed Jordan a couple of favors, but I ain't so sure this is the time to do any paying back."

Fontana smiled in relief. He liked the lawman, wanted no trouble with him—and trouble there would be if Locke tried to stop him.

"Obliged to you, Marshal," he said. "Tell you again I'm right sorry about Beaver."

"Was bound to happen sooner or later," Locke replied. "You riding on?"

"In the morning," Fontana said, and swung his attention to Yeager. "Going over now and get something to eat. After that I'm crawling into bed at the hotel. That's where I'll be, and if you've still got it in your head to take me back to Agua Prieta, you best be holding both of those fancy guns you're wearing, cocked and ready to use when you come after me. That clear?"

Yeager, his face a bright red, made no answer. Fontana moved away from the table, started for the door. He paused, looked back.

"Same goes for in the morning. I'll be lining out for El Paso about sunrise. You try dogging me and I'll put lead in you. Want you to understand that, too."

The lawman's features were grim set, his eyes hard. The deputy clung to a tight-lipped silence.

"You hear?" Fontana demanded.

This time Yeager answered. Nodding his head, he muttered, "Sure—I'm listening."

"Believe it, too," Fontana snapped, and continued on his way.

• 21 •

Fontana drew the black in sharply as three riders appeared suddenly and blocked his path. They had come from the hidden side of one of the many small buttes through which the trail carved its course. It was mid-afternoon and he had made the long ride from Las Cruces with no problems, Deputy Bill Yeager evidently having heeded the warning served him.

Hat pulled low over his eyes, he studied the men narrowly. . . . A big, wide-shouldered individual wearing a lead-gray business suit, the pant legs of which were tucked inside black stovepipe boots that came to his knees; two younger riders, one obviously a Mexican. Each had a star pinned conspicuously to the pocket of his shirt. . . . El Paso lawmen. . . .

Fontana glanced about. There was nothing but open country around him—no trees, no brush of consequence into which he could wheel, quickly lose them and continue his journey uninterrupted to the border settlement, now only a short distance ahead. After a time he sighed, put the gelding in motion and moved on. The big man in the center allowed him to draw close, then raised his hand.

"Fontana?"

Surprised, the lawman again halted. "That's me."

"Been expecting you. Got word by stagecoach this morning you were heading this way. . . . I'll take those warrants you're carrying."

Yeager again. Apparently the deputy had dropped a letter in the mail the previous night advising the El Paso sheriff of his intentions. Fontana shook his head.

"They stay with me."

"You're in Texas now. Warrants're no good—and I ain't putting up with no killings."

"Warrants I've got are good anywhere. Far as killing goes, that's up to the outlaws I'm after.".

The El Paso lawman brushed at the sweat on his weath-

103

ered features. The heat was intense, a solid, withering force hanging sullenly over the rocky basin in which the town lay.

"Any hunting down and arresting around here'll be done by me or my deputies—not no outsider. What's the names on them papers?"

"Won't mean anything to you. Been changed."

"I'll listen to them, anyway."

John Fontana's shoulders moved slightly in resignation. "One's a youngster, name of Wayne Vetch. Another is Shorty Reece. All I've ever heard him called, Shorty."

"The third?"

"Bart Fontana."

The sheriff frowned, glanced at his deputies. The Mexican wagged his head wonderingly.

"He some kin to you?" the lawman asked.

"Brother."

The young Anglo deputy leaned forward. "You aim to gun him down like you done all them others?"

"It comes to it, I will."

The sheriff spat. "From what I hear, it always seems to come to it. You've caught up with four of the seven you're chasing, and there's been three of them that had to be planted. I'm thinking you're maybe a mite too handy with that iron you pack."

"Killed some yahoo up Cruces way, too, that letter said," the young deputy observed.

Fontana irritably sleeved away the sweat on his face. "Friend, we have to sit here in the sun like this? If you figure to keep on talking, let's go to your office. Expect you've got one."

"Reckon I have," the lawman drawled. "And don't be calling me friend. Ain't so sure I like the idea. The name's Kidd. This here deputy's called Earl and the *vaquero* is Lopez."

Fontana acknowledged the introductions with only a small change in his eyes. Earl was little more than a boy, eighteen at the most. Lopez was older, appeared to regard all things with amusement.

"Supposing you just come over here and get in the middle, then we'll all ride into town."

Fontana swung the gelding into the space created for him. Earl leaned forward, reached for the gun on the lawman's leg.

"I'll take that—"

"Not unless you're tired of living," Fontana cut in coldly.

The deputy drew back, glanced questioningly at Kidd. The sheriff shrugged, turned away. Lopez only smiled in his dark, enigmatic way.

They formed a line four abreast, with Fontana and the older lawman in the center, deputies flanking, and moved on.

"You know where to find these jaspers you're after?" Kidd asked in a more conciliatory tone.

"No. Could be they're not even here—only think they are from what I've been told. Been some time since they headed in this direction."

"There something special about them that'll put a tag on them?"

"Not much. Probably lay around a saloon and do a lot of gambling. Had plenty of money when they started out."

"New gold that letter said. How much?"

"Five thousand in double-eagles. They would've split it seven ways. Then there was paper and silver added to that."

Kidd whistled softly. "Ought to make a few folks set up and notice them—throwing that kind of money around!"

"Was the gold that's made it easier to track them. Brand new double-eagles. Man they took them from had just got them from the mint."

Sheriff Kidd had made no mention of his trouble with the Mexican authorities. Being a border lawman in the same position as Jordan at Agua Prieta, he likely felt the same obligation to the Mexican officials. He was intentionally avoiding the subject, Fontana realized, and that could mean only one thing; he had plans in mind.

Again mopping away sweat, the lawman glanced about. They were entering the town now, passing along a wide, dusty street on which houses stood at irregular intervals. There were a few trees to be seen, an occasional dusty shrub, but the heat was no less oppressive.

Farther on he could see a tight cluster of buildings—the main part of El Paso, he supposed, and weighed the wisdom of accompanying the sheriff and his deputies any farther, much less into the confines of his office and jail.

Abruptly he halted, let his broad hand fall upon the butt of his pistol. Facing Kidd, he said: "Am I going to have trouble with you, Sheriff? If so, we'll settle it now."

The Texan looked startled. Earl and Lopez wheeled slowly about, features stilled. Kidd brushed nervously at his mustache, his chin.

"Well, now, I ain't—"

"I'll tell you what you ain't," Fontana snapped, "you're not getting in my way. If you don't want somebody hurt you'll keep that in mind."

"You threatening me?" the lawman demanded in a blustering voice.

"Only giving you a little advice. Nobody's going to keep me from doing what I have to do."

"I won't stand for no killings in my town!"

"Won't be any unless I'm forced into it. I find the men I'm trailing, I'll give them their chance to give up. They decide they want to argue with me about it with a gun, then likely it'll end up the other way."

Kidd continued to claw at his chin. "Well, putting it that way, I reckon I can't put up no fuss. I got your word on it?"

"You have."

Earl swore angrily. "You believing him? You letting him put us off by just saying that?"

The sheriff nodded. "Lawman same as us, ain't he?"

"Not so damn sure. All them killings——"

Fontana relaxed gently, smiled at the younger man. "Being the law's not all parading around town showing off how big you are," he said. "Day comes when you have to live up to the meaning of that badge you're wearing—like it or not."

The *vaquero's* teeth showed whitely between his lips. *"Es verdad, senor.* Sometimes it is a matter for the gun."

Fontana made no comment, but he felt a little closer to the Mexican. He appeared to have a better understanding than either Kidd or Earl—but he was a Mexican and his sympathies could lie with Rodriguez and Ortega and the other officials at Agua Prieta.

"One thing more, if you've got any ideas about doing Jordan a favor, taking me back to him——"

"Jordan?" Kidd echoed. "Oh, yeh, there was some mentioning him in that letter from that fellow Yeager. Well, that's their business with you and I reckon we'll just leave it that way. . . . That's my office over there," he finished, pointing to a building set back somewhat from the street. "You want to pull up, cool off a mite?"

Fontana shook his head. "As soon go on about my job. Where you figure I'd be most apt to find this bunch I'm after?"

The sheriff again fell to smoothing his mustache. "Most of the big gambling's done at the Texas Star. It'd be my guess."

"Where is it?"

"Straight on till you get to the end of the street. Border's there. Can tell it by the wire fence. You'll see the Texas Star on your left. . . . You sure you don't want some help?"

"I need any I'll send word," Fontana replied, and rode on.

• 22 •

Few were abroad in the blast-furnace heat gripping El Paso. Here and there a man dozed in the shadows, back to a wall, head tipped forward. Dogs panted in the scanty shade, inert, uninterested. No sound broke the breathless hush except the shrill buzz of cicadas.

John Fontana gave it all little note as he walked the black slowly down the length of the street and veered toward the hitchrack at the side of the Texas Star Saloon. The end of the long trail was at hand, the moment he had looked forward to, yet subconsciously mistrusted, was upon him.

Jaw set, he dismounted, circled the low, squat structure to its entrance, standing open in the vain hope of capturing a vagrant breeze that might pass that way, and stepped inside. Attendance was good, possibly because the two-foot-thick adobe walls made for a marked coolness and offered refuge from the savage outdoor temperature.

A dozen men stood at the bar, their features reflected in the long mirror gracing the back section. An area to the right, separated from the bar by an arch from which dangled a series of dusty tassels, once red, was reserved for gambling. It, too, had its share of listless patrons.

Fontana, methodically reviewing the faces in the glow of several wagonwheel chandeliers, brought his gaze to a halt at a table where blackjack was being played. Grim satisfaction spread through him. The young cotton-haired dealer was Wayne Vetch.

After a few moments the lawman resumed his search of the room, completed it, made a second visual quest. Bart and Shorty Reece were not present. It didn't matter; Vetch would tell him where they could be found.

Ignoring the bartender, Fontana crossed the width of the saloon, stepped down into the casino area, and threaded his way to the blackjack table. The solitary player looked up into the lawman's bleak face as he halted closeby, hastily gathered up his money, and moved off. Vetch, engaged in stacking the coins in front of him, finally raised his glance. His eyes spread in alarm as he involuntarily jerked back.

"Try running and I'll kill you," Fontana said in an even voice. "I'm taking you in."

The outlaw remained rigid in his chair, fear immobilizing him. Elsewhere in the Texas Star business proceeded uninterrupted.

The lawman, hand resting on the butt of his pistol, circled the table. "Stand up."

Vetch rose slowly. Fontana looked him over critically for a weapon. The outlaw shook his head.

"I ain't armed."

It was probably a lie; likely he had a hide-out gun somewhere on his person. He would bear close watching, Fontana decided, until there was a better opportunity to search.

"Where's Bart and Reece?"

A sly expression came over Vetch's face. "How the hell should I know?"

Anger, so carefully controlled from the moment he had first spotted the killer, began to glow within the lawman. His mouth was a straight line, barely opening.

"They came here with you."

"Who said?" Vetch countered coyly. His confidence seemed to rise with the knowledge that his partners were yet free.

"Makes no difference who—I'm asking you where they are."

"And I'll fry in hell before I tell you," the outlaw declared boldly.

The words had scarcely left his lips when Fontana's hand shot out, grasped him by the shirt front, and jerked him forward.

"You'll talk!" the lawman snarled, and slammed Vetch hard into the wall behind him.

A shout went up in the room as the outlaw crashed against the solid, mud-brick partition, rebounded into the table. It upset noisily, spilling coins and cards to the floor and knocking over two chairs.

Raging, the lawman seized Vetch by the throat and belt buckle, lifted him bodily off his feet, threw him again into the unyielding wall. The outlaw's head struck with a sickening thud. He sagged, crumpled.

Behind him Fontana could hear the scuff of boots as the saloon's customers began to hurriedly collect. Some were protesting indignantly the treatment being accorded the blackjack dealer, others simply voicing questions. Paying no heed, the lawman stepped to where Vetch lay, yanked him upright, and slapped him viciously across the face.

A threatening howl lifted from the crowd. Someone said: "Goddammit—I don't know what he done to you, mister, but he ain't deserving of getting a beating like that!"

"Hell, no!" another voice cried. "You can at least give the man a chance!"

Fontana released his grip on Vetch, whirled to face the room. His eyes were flaming and his massive frame trembled with fury.

"A man—him? He's nothing but filth! Ask him about all those folks he killed in a town called Genesis. Ask him about the two young girls and their ma, and what he and six more just like him did to them one day! Ask him about the gold they stole and how they burned that town to the ground —wiped it off the map. Ask him all that, then see if you figure he ought to be called a man!"

Silence had descended upon the smoke-filled saloon. Vetch groaned deeply. Fontana spun once again, seized the outlaw, dragged him upright, and turning, flung him at the crowd.

"Ask him—you bunch of bleeding hearts!" he shouted as the pack of onlookers surged back. "Ask him!"

A man in the front line, possessed by a measure of practicality, considered the outlaw shrewdly. "Shape he's in he ain't able to answer nothing. . . . How come you know all this about Amos?"

"Amos!" Fontana spat at the sprawled figure. "His name's Vetch—Wayne Vetch."

"Been calling hisself Amos Jay around here. You ain't said how you know—"

"I was the marshal of that town, that's how. Was seven of them, seven just like him. Soon as I was able I started tracking them. Got four—he makes number five, and he knows where the other two are."

"There was a 'couple of fellows with him when he first blew in." It was one of the bartenders. "Recollect them hanging around together. Then they was gone. Heard later from somebody they'd gone across the line to Juarez, got themselves in a big game, and cleaned up a pile of money."

"What happened after that?"

The saloonman wagged his head. "Sure don't know, Marshal."

"Well, he does," Fontana snarled, and stepping to where Vetch lay, pulled him to his feet. "Aim to get it out of him!"

Dropping back, he shoved the stunned outlaw against the wall once more. "You ready to talk?"

"Maybe was we to get a rope, do a little stringing up," someone suggested.

"Sure—fetch a rope!"

The crowd's sympathies had shifted, now lay with the lawman. More yells went up approving the suggestion.

"You hear that, Vetch?" Fontana pressed, holding the man tight against the adobes. "They're bringing a rope. Better talk."

The outlaw struggled weakly in Fontana's relentless grip, recoiled as the lawman slapped him sharply.

"Talk!"

Vetch bobbed frantically. "All right—all right! They ain't here."

"Know that. Where'd they go?"

"Town up in the panhandle," the outlaw gasped. "Bought themselves a saloon—gambling house."

Fontana shook the man violently. "Town—what town? Lot of them up that way."

Vetch's head wobbled loosely. "Mescalero. . . . For God's sake don't—"

The lawman released his grip on the outlaw, drew his pistol. Jamming the barrel into the man's back, he pushed him forward and looked out over the crowd.

"Told me what I wanted to know. Going to turn him over to the sheriff now."

A howl of objection arose as the crowd pushed forward.

"What about using this here rope?" a man yelled, waving his lariat aloft.

"Wouldn't make much difference to me," Fontana replied. "Dead's dead, but I gave my word to Kidd."

Reaching out he gave Vetch a shove, sent him stumbling ahead. "Step back—everybody!"

The wall of onlookers did not break. From somewhere in the back a voice shouted: "If he done all them things you claim he did, he don't deserve no trial!"

"He'll get one," the lawman snapped, and raising his weapon, fired a shot into the ceiling.

Immediately the crowd gave way, parted, leaving a corridor for the scar-faced lawman and his prisoner. Fontana shepherded the outlaw down its length to the doorway and out into the burning sunlight, then paused to look back. The men in the saloon, stilled by the utter violence of the lawman, were making no move to follow.

Turning right, Fontana continued on to where the black waited, and there, taking his rope, shook out a loop and placed it about Vetch's body. That done he climbed onto the saddle and pointed to the upper end of the street.

"Sheriff's office is that way," he said. His anger had now faded and once again he was restrained and deceptively intense. "Start walking. Hold back and I'll drag you."

Kidd and his deputies, becoming aware of his approach, were waiting in front of the jail when he reached there with his prisoner. All stared in surprise but only the sheriff spoke.

"This him? Hell, he's been around here for quite a spell. Calls himself—"

"Name's Vetch no matter what he says," Fontana cut in, dismounting and freeing his rope. "Handing him over to you and holding you responsible for him."

"He'll be here," Kidd said brusquely, motioning to Lopez to take charge of the prisoner. "You got that warrant?"

Fontana selected it from those remaining in his leather packet, passed it over. Considering thoughtfully the three remaining, he removed the one covering Buckram also, and borrowing the lawman's pencil, scrawled DEAD across its surface."

"Be obliged if you'll send that along to the marshal when you notify him," he said, surrendering it.

Kidd nodded. "What about them other two? He say they were here?"

"No," the lawman answered, coiling his rope. "Up the panhandle way. Town called Mescalero."

"Heard of it," the sheriff said, pursing his lips. "Sort of new. Trail town, I think."

"You heading for there now?" Earl asked.

"Soon as I get a bite to eat," Fontana replied, returning the lariat to his saddle. "Restaurant around here close?"

"Back down the street a piece," Kidd said. "Getting late. Might as well lay over till morning. Can bunk at my place."

"Appreciate that," Fontana said, "but I figure to get this over with. Had hoped it would end here but it didn't. Now, the sooner I get to this Mescalero, the quicker it will. . . . Obliged to you."

Kidd bobbed his head. "Luck," he murmured, and went back into his office.

An hour later John Fontana rode out of the sweltering crucible in which the settlement of El Paso lay, and turned his flat-planed, inflexible face to the north.

It occurred to him as he pulled up onto a wide, brush-covered plateau that he had not asked the distance to Mescalero, but it was of small importance. It was in that lengthy, wind-swept neck known as the panhandle, and he would have no difficulty locating it in that area. In any event, it would take days—a week or more, probably; Texas was a seemingly endless expanse of land.

Five down, two to go—and one would be Bart. He had thought the inevitable moment of confrontation was on hand in El Paso, but luck or fate, which ever it was, had ruled otherwise; now it lay again in the future. Fontana shook his head, refusing to dwell on the matter. He'd not think about it, not let it disturb him. He'd deal with Bart the same as he had the others.

Motion some distance ahead, at the edge of a rocky, brush-covered wash through which the road wound, caught his close attention. He drew in the black, conscious of the warning sounding within himself. There was someone there, waiting at the narrow passage between the rocks. It had been the hindquarters of a horse swinging out of sight that he had seen.

Indians? Comanches or perhaps Kiowas, or it could be Apaches. They were a little too near El Paso and its army post; that it could be a party of marauding braves didn't seem likely. Road agents? He grinned at the idea. They would find him mighty slim pickings. He was down to his last double-eagle. Regardless, he was not about to ride straight into their hands, let them stop him, perhaps steal his horse, and at best delay him for a time.

He glanced about. A smaller draw cut off to his right. At once he swung into it, followed its curving course for a half mile or so. Finally, reckoning that he should be somewhere east of the arroyo where the road lay, he turned north. Continuing on through a welter of greasewood, rabbitbush, and snakeweed, he kept his attention to the west, and shortly reached a point where he could see the trail where it passed between the rocks.

The lawman halted. There were three men. They had dismounted, were standing two on one side, the third on the opposite side, of the entrance into the arroyo. Temper lifted within him as he recognized them. Kidd's deputies, Earl and Lopez—and Bill Yeager from Agua Prieta.

Yeager had followed him down from Las Cruces after all, had made himself scarce during the time in El Paso, and then recruiting the aid of the two Texas deputies, had ridden out to ambush him. Fontana's hand drifted slowly to the pistol on his hip, settled upon its worn handle. They needed a lesson, all of them—especially Bill Yeager.

A moment later the anger passed. They were young, probably thought they were doing right. Let it pass. Let them stand there baking and sweating in the driving sun; that in itself would be a sufficient lesson. Besides, it was the last he'd ever see of them and there'd already been enough trouble—and too much killing.

• 23 •

There was always something singularly lonely about a Sunday morning in a strange town. John Fontana, slouched on the porch of the hotel in which he'd spent the night, moodily considered the dusty street with its tightly closed houses, its arching sycamores and chinaberries, their leaves absolutely still in the windless air, and felt the deep, thrusting emptiness of the moment.

The settlement was well-named, he thought—Prairieview. In all directions, as far as the eye could see, there was nothing but flat land, interrupted only occasionally by a home with its close scatter of outbuildings and cluster of carefully planted and nurtured trees. Some were devoted to cattle raising, others to general farming, but regardless of purpose, all presented the same unyielding face of independence and isolation to the outer world.

He was two days short of Mescalero. It had been his plan to stay the night in Prairieview, which appeared to be an emerald smear in the shimmering distance, and ride on the following morning. Long before he reached it, however, it became apparent that the hard-pressed black would have to be granted a day's rest. Never fully regaining his strength after that day Fontana had ridden him out of Agua Prieta, and no more than a mediocre horse at best, he was in danger of caving in unless given a respite.

Now, eyes traveling restlessly over the neat white houses along the shady lane, each seemingly devoid of life in the unbroken hush, the lawman was at a loss as to what he could do with the hours that stretched before him.

He was unwilling to think of what waited for him at Mescalero—Bart, Shorty Reece, and the violence that was sure to come. His mind was weary of such, rebelled at the consideration. Inwardly he was bone-tired of all things, sick of the chase, of bloodshed, of riding the empty trails, of going nowhere and having nothing.

The quiet and peace of the little town magnified the feel-

ing, pointed up the futility of his being, and filled him with a
need he could not exactly comprehend. There had to be more
to life than he was experiencing, a voice within him seemed
to be saying—yet he had followed that same voice for all of
his life, from mid-boyhood to that day; why was he questioning it now?

Was it the fact that like an angel of death he was stalking
the last of his intended victims, that before many more sun-
downs he would likely add two more names to the list of
men he had been compelled to gun down—and one of those
his own brother?

Tallent . . . Buckram . . . Bill Glade . . . that man in Las
Cruces, Jud—strange he could not remember his last name.
Now there would be two others. . . . Fontana stirred impatiently. Why was he feeling sorry for them? They had it
coming, deserved no consideration. As for himself, it was his
job, his sworn duty whether he liked it or not. But maybe
such was beginning to wear on him; maybe he ought to
think about turning in his star, find another way of life.

He'd forgotten what peace was like. The hushed street, the
silent houses, the motionless trees, yards in which flowers
bloomed behind picket fences while lilacs perfumed the air.
All such closed softly about John Fontana, disturbing him,
causing him to think, to remember what once he'd hoped to
be. The bitterness of what he was surfaced in him, like the
ugly slime that floated to the top of a backwater pool.

He would be forever branded now, respected perhaps but
an outcast to be feared and avoided by the very people he
placed his life on the line to protect. It was ironical; without
him and his kind they could not survive, yet they set him
apart, accepted him into their homes reluctantly and only
out of a sense of duty. It had been so even in Genesis, it
would be no different in the next town—if there was to be
a next town.

Somewhere down the street a child called out, broke the
stillness. Another answered. Shortly a small girl in starchy
white trimmed with lace, leading a smaller, sober-faced boy
in dark knee pants, jacket, and wide-collared shirt, came into
view. They were joined by a second youngster emerging from
the house opposite, and then together, hand in hand, they
started for the steepled church farther down the way.

The bell in the prim little structure began to ring, the
clean, clear sound echoing sweetly as it rocked back and

forth between the houses. Men and women and more children began to appear. Clad in their Sabbath best, they strolled toward the church in obedience to the summons. It was that day in Genesis all over again; the people, the bell, the hush—how long ago was it now? Two months—more, going onto three. It could have been only yesterday.

The pealing slowed, died to a final tap. The street again became empty, silent. Fontana, roused for that brief time from the depths of the dark thoughts that had claimed him, slipped once more into his melancholy mood, and then on sudden impulse stepped off the hotel porch and moved slowly toward the church.

It had been years since he had attended services and there was no inclination now to break the practice; it was simply a need to be around, even if just near, people other than those he was forced to associate with and perhaps later have to kill.

He reached the churchyard, a distance back from the street. A dozen buggies and carriages were tied up at the racks along with a few saddled horses. From the open door of the small building the strains of a hymn began to pour out, led by a strong baritone voice and a well-played piano.

Fontana moved on to the corner of the structure, leaned against its clapboard wall. The music ceased, was followed by a prayer at low voice. A second hymn, more lively than the first, began. It came to an end and the baritone voice took over, speaking strong, but the words were still unintelligible to the lawman.

He appeared not to mind, continued to stand in the shade cast by the trees encircling the yard, eyes half closed, features expressionless. Off in the fields below, meadowlarks whistled cheerfully, and from some nearby watering pond the unmistakable call of bobolinks reached him.

The speaking broke off, another prayer, and then once more the notes of a joyous hymn. Morose, Fontana remained motionless, and then became aware that the music no longer filled the warm air, that persons were coming into the open, gathering in groups, talking, exchanging news and gossip.

Trapped, the lawman waited for the gathering to disperse, feeling more the outcast, the outsider than ever. He glanced toward the gate hopefully, saw instead a woman, tall, well-proportioned, with smooth, attractive features and a wealth of dark hair. It was capped by a pearl gray bonnet secured under her chin by a ribbon that matched the blue of the dress she wore.

She regarded him intently, and in return, he nodded, touched the brim of his hat with a forefinger. Immediately she moved toward him, a smile on her lips.

"You're a stranger here," she said, halting.

Fontana pulled off his hat, pleased that he had troubled to shave and put on clean clothing that morning.

"Yes, ma'm. Passing through."

"I'm Marissa Hale," she continued, offering a slender hand. "We're always glad to welcome newcomers to Prairieview."

There was something wistful in her manner. It was as if she were one alone, too, and recognizing the same in him, sought out a kindred soul.

"A nice town," the lawman murmured, enclosing her hand in his. It was warm, soft, had the feel of great gentleness.

"Are you here alone—or is—your wife—"

"Alone," he said, releasing her. "No wife."

"I'm by myself, too. A widow."

It was an awkward moment, one that found Fontana at a loss for words. Finally he murmured, "Sorry to hear that."

She smiled brightly. "It was a long time ago. Three years to be exact. The hurt's gone, but not the—" She hesitated, glanced to the front of the yard. The congregation was beginning to move on, some drifting slowly toward the carriages, others for the street.

"Will you be staying the day?" she asked, bringing her attention back to him.

"Till morning. Had to rest up my horse."

Her features brightened. "Then—I wonder, would you care to have Sunday dinner with me? I—I had planned on guests but they were forced to cancel. I would love it if you—"

Fontana nodded. "Be my pleasure, Mrs. Hale."

"Marissa—please!" she said, and laughing, reached for his arm.

"Long as you call me by my first name, too. It's John."

"John it will be. Shall we go? I live just down the street a ways."

Fontana hesitated briefly. "You sure this'll be all right, you taking up with a stranger and treating him to a dinner? Won't folks talk?"

Marissa tossed her head. "I'm tired of worrying about

what others will do, and I won't let it bother me. I think people should live their lives the way they want, don't you?"

John Fontana shrugged. "If there's a choice," he said quietly as they moved on.

• 24 •

Marissa's house was a neat, well-kept bungalow placed some distance back from the street. There were flowers everywhere, and a huge chinaberry spread its branches overhead, shielding all from the sun. In back Fontana could see a small garden—a half a dozen rows of corn, squash, onions, cabbage, some kind of melon.

As she opened the door and led him into a parlor, dustless and precise in its arrangement of dark furniture, antimacassars, framed pictures on the papered walls, deep green carpet with red roses forming a border, he nodded approvingly.

"A fine place—a home," he said. "The kind that sets a man to thinking."

Marissa Hale smiled, removed her bonnet and carried it into an adjoining room. He had a glimpse of a cushioned rocking chair, a mirror hung above a table, a bed with a snowy white cover.

"It's really not a home," she said, returning. "It takes two to make it that. . . . Won't you come on out into the kitchen? Coffee needs only heating—and there's a peach pie. You can eat a piece with your coffee while I get things ready."

The lawman followed her down a short hallway into a combination kitchen and dining area. He halted in the doorway, looked around. Marissa turned to him, apology in her eyes.

"I wasn't expecting anybody," she said. "I lied to you—I just couldn't go through another Sunday alone. . . . When I saw you standing there at the corner of the church you looked as lonely as I felt. That gave me the courage to ask you."

"Easy for me to understand," he said with a wry smile. "And I'm glad you did."

Marissa regarded him soberly for a long moment, and then motioning to one of the chairs placed about a table in the corner, turned to the stove. Setting the enameled coffee

120

pot on a back lid, she removed a forward one, poked the fire within to life.

"Loneliness can be a terrible thing," she said without looking up.

"You learn to live with it."

"I wonder. . . . I thought I could, but lately—" Her words broke off and then she continued. "What kind of work do you do, John?"

"Lawman. Leastwise that's what I am now. Done a few other things."

"Are you from around here somewhere?"

"New Mexico. On my way to a town north of here, Mescalero."

"I've heard of it," she said, taking a large pie from the stove's warming oven. Placing it on a nearby work table, she reached for a saucer and knife, carved out a wedge and set it before him. "You must be going there after somebody."

"Two outlaws," he replied, and added, "one's my brother."

Staring at him, she sank into the chair opposite. "Oh, John—I'm—"

"No call to be sorry," he cut in brusquely. "He's a murderer, the worst kind, and he'll hang when I get him back to Santa Fe, or I'll kill him now if he wants to put up a fight."

Somehow he felt better for having said it. All along it had been there in his mind, and there had been times when he'd mentioned it aloud, but only piecemeal. Now it was all laid out—complete.

He studied the woman silently, assessing her reaction. It was one not so much of horror as of sympathy. At once he felt himself warming to her; Marissa had a depth of understanding far greater than he had expected, or could ever hope for.

"I guess duty can be a terrible thing, too," she murmured, and rising, took up the now simmering coffee pot. Getting cups and saucers, she again sat down at the table.

"Are you afraid of what you have to do? I—I don't mean afraid of him. I don't think you'd ever be afraid of any man —I mean, since he is your brother?"

She had put her finger on it exactly. "Reckon I am. Just not sure what it'll be like when the time comes," he said slowly. "Been wondering if I'll hold back."

"Be only natural. Can't you let some other lawman do it for you?"

Fontana shook his head, took a sip of the coffee. It was

strong, black, the way he liked it. "Was my fault they done what they did. If I'd listened to the other folks in my town, made them move on, it never would've happened. But he was my brother and I trusted him, let him and his bunch stay. Makes me responsible and leaves it up to me to see that it's finished."

"There were several of them?"

"Seven. I've squared for all but my brother and the one with him."

There was a time of silence. Out in the back, starlings were quarreling in the chinaberry tree, and nearby a woman was singing as she prepared the noon meal for her family. The words of the popular war melody floated softly on the still air—*the years creep slowly by, Lorena.* . . .

"Squared—does that mean—"

"Killed three of them. Got two locked up waiting for the U.S. marshal."

That was out, too, and again he had a feeling of relief.

"I'm sure you did what you had to," Marissa said.

Again she rose, crossed to the stove, and removing the lid from a large kettle, poked about in its contents with a long-handled spoon.

"It'll be ready soon," she said. "We're having a boiled dinner—beef, potatoes, along with all the other vegetables."

Fontana watched her as she moved about. A quietness had come over her, almost a sadness, but he could think of nothing to say that would lighten the moments. She finished at the stove, turned to a glass-fronted wall cabinet, selected plates, smaller dishes, and silverware, distributed them upon the table. Abruptly she faced him.

"John, I think you should let some other lawman do it for you."

"My job. Got to see it through."

"But it's wrong! You shouldn't expect it of yourself. The scars it will leave inside you won't ever go away."

Unthinking, his fingers sought the bullet trace along his cheek. Marissa shook her head. "That kind doesn't matter. The ones within you do."

"You can learn to live with them, too," he said woodenly.

She sighed, served up the meal, and they ate with minimal and desultory conversation. When it was over, he waited until she had cleared the table of dishes and then both repaired to the backyard, where chairs had been placed in the shade.

"Did you say you would be riding on in the morning?"

The lawman nodded. "One day, all the time I can spare. Wouldn't have taken that if my horse had been in better shape."

"I see. . . . When it's all over at Mescalero, will you go back to New Mexico?"

"Maybe. Not sure. Lot depends on how things turn out. . . . Don't have a job anymore. My town's gone."

"Gone?" Marissa looked puzzled.

"They burned it to the ground. Folks there lost everything, moved on." He hesitated, gaze reaching out beyond the yard to the clear, hot sky above, where a flock of crows were etched against the blue. "Had a job offered me."

"Something other than a lawman?" she asked quickly, hopefully.

"No. I'd be the U.S. marshal—deputy. In Santa Fe. Not sure I want it. Think maybe I'll start doing something else—don't know exactly what."

"You'd find something once you make up your mind that you're through being a lawman."

"What I know best."

"But you could do other work. I'm certain of it unless—"

John Fontana glanced up. "Unless?"

"Unless you like doing what you have to do—the shooting—hunting—"

He gave that thought. "Could be, but I don't think so."

"Then quit it, John! Give it up before it's too late. I can see what it's doing to you, and now with this thing about your brother—"

"That's not going to make a difference. I'll handle him same as if he was a stranger. Aim to jail him if I can; if he puts up a fight, I'll have to kill him."

There was no harsh determination in his voice, only a bitter resignation, the reluctant admission of a fact that he must face. Marissa sighed deeply.

"I wish you would listen to me, let someone else be the one to arrest him. I'm afraid."

He studied her closely. "It matter to you? I'm no more than a stranger."

She made a small gesture with her hands. "How long does it take to become friends—or more than just friends? Only minutes if two people meet who are right for each other. It matters a great deal to me. Everything, in fact."

Fontana looked away. "Thought maybe it was all on my

part," he murmured and fell silent. After a time he added, "Can't be thinking about that—us—now. When it's all over and done with we can talk."

Marissa lowered her head. He leaned forward, laid his hand on hers. "No cause to be worrying."

"I will though. I can't help it. I loved my husband very much, and lost him. I don't want to be hurt again."

"I'll come through it."

"Maybe you will, but if you keep on being a lawman, nothing will change. I'll always be afraid for you. I know we have to have men doing that job—but for our sake, won't you leave it to others? You've done your part."

"We'll talk about it later."

"If there is a later."

"There will be," he said quietly, and got to his feet. "Can we get on some other subject? Saw a guitar there in your parlor. You play it?"

Marissa smiled, brushed at her eyes. "After a fashion. I'll play if you'll sing."

He grinned self-consciously, never having been called upon to do so before. "Not sure what'll come out when I open my mouth, but I'm willing."

She grasped his hand, came upright quickly, and turned for the door. There was a light-heartedness to her, a happiness that glowed in her eyes. Fontana allowed himself to be pulled into the house, some of her gaiety infecting him, loosening the grim set of his lips, and through his mind passed the thought: *this is what living is really like. This is what I've been missing all these years.*

• 25 •

John Fontana put it all behind him, out of his mind—Marissa, a home, a happy, normal way of life in which there would be no loneliness; he could not permit himself to think of those things now.

He was a lawman. He could not afford sentiment any more than he could allow the sweet and gentle dreams Marissa Hale evoked in him to color his thoughts. . . . Think now of only the past, of what had transpired in Genesis. Think of the men who had died, the women who had suffered; remember the dry, scorched smell of a doomed town going up in flames. The recollection of such, to the exclusion of all else, was what would be required in the moments that lay ahead—moments in which he could be called upon to kill his own brother.

Standing on the corner opposite the Highroller Saloon in Mescalero late the second day after leaving Prairieview, Fontana shook off the tension that gripped him and stepped out into the dusty street, restless with trail riders, homeward-bound chuckwagons, and other pilgrims. Crossing, he mounted the saloon's porch, ignoring the local marshal, who paused in his conversation with several men to give him a speculative glance, and entered.

It was noisy, smoke-filled, and enjoying a good patronage. Halting just within the swinging doors, he glanced about the room, stiffened slowly. Bart and Shorty Reece, dressed in expensive clothing, enjoying slim black cigars, were seated at a table in the back. Hovering nearby, round, dark eyes darting back and forth, arms folded across his chest, was a man Fontana recalled from past years, a gunslinger called Donovan. Evidently Bart and Shorty had felt it necessary, in their new prominence, to employ a hired gun.

Cool, determination a leveling force within him, Fontana pushed into the milling crowd, worked his way through until he reached the corner where his brother and Shorty Reece

125

sat. Unnoticed, back to them, he eased in closer, stopped, seemingly a man looking out over the room, absorbing the sounds and smells. Abruptly he wheeled.

"I've come for you two!" he snapped.

Bart's eyes flared in surprise. Reece rocked back, dragged at the gun he was wearing. Fontana drew fast, fired point blank, spun, triggered a second bullet into Donovan—from the edge of his vision he had seen the man go for his weapon. The gunman slammed back against the wall, fell forward.

As the shattering echoes died, Fontana stared through the drifting smoke at his brother, motionless in his chair, hands raised.

"I'm taking you back to hang," the lawman said, his voice audible throughout the hushed saloon. "Can make it easy or you can try your hand same as Shorty—and a couple of the others."

Bart smiled. "Sure surprised to see you, kid."

"So were the others. . . . What's it to be?"

The older man shrugged. "Seeing as how we're brothers, you don't need to be asking. Wouldn't be right, us shooting at each other."

"Wasn't the way you looked at it back in Genesis."

"Couldn't help that—and it wasn't me. Rest of the boys just plain went crazy. Real sorry about it."

John Fontana relaxed gently but the coldness remained. "All right, let's go. You give me trouble and I'll—"

"Hell, I ain't going to give my own kid brother no trouble. Besides, I know when I'm beat," Bart said, rising slowly.

"Move out here—"

"Sure, sure. It jake with you if I put my hands down? You can see I ain't wearing iron."

Fontana nodded, turned to step back, allow his prisoner to get in front of him. In that same fragment of time he saw Bart's arm jerk suddenly. A shrill warning raced through him. He spun to the side, came up fast, froze as a gun blasted from somewhere in the forefront of the crowd.

Bart, a snub-nosed Derringer clutched in his hand, staggered against the table, a tight smile on his lips. He hung there briefly, staring eyes fixed on Fontana, and then fell across the body of Shorty Reece.

An exhaustion filling him, Fontana came about, faced the crowd. A man, pistol still in his hand was coming toward him. . . . The marshal he had noticed on the saloon's porch.

"Name's Curry," he said. "Had you figured for a lawman when I seen you outside. Can spot one every time. Reckon I showed up just right. . . . Where you hail from?"

"New Mexico," Fontana replied, reaching inside his shirt for the last two warrants. Handing them to Curry, he looked down at Bart. It was all over, finished, and his brother was dead but not a victim of his gun. It was better that way, he guessed. Marissa had said—

"These here names on the papers, they ain't what that pair was calling themselves around here, but that don't surprise me none," Curry said. "Always figured there was something wrong about them. . . . Another thing. Warrants say your name's Fontana, and one of them in there's named Fontana. He some kin?"

"Was."

Marshal Curry was a small, thin man with sandy hair, quick, birdlike movements, and a mustache that was much too large for his features. He studied Fontana, who rose head and shoulders above him in thoughtful silence. Patrons of the saloon were crowding by the two men, seeking a closer look at the dead outlaws.

Curry shrugged. "Well, I reckon that's the way it goes sometimes for us lawmen," he said, and waggled the papers in his hand. "What do you want me to do with these?"

"Write dead across them and sign your name. Got to return them to Santa Fe."

The load had lifted from John Fontana. It was all over, he told himself again. He could now start thinking of other things, of the decision that must be made—of Marissa and the future. He smiled at Curry.

"Want to thank you for taking a hand when you did."

"Ain't no thanks needed. Us lawmen got to stick together. . . . You know, it's a dang good thing there's jaspers like us willing to take on the job of clamping down on scum like them laying there. If there wasn't, this country'd never get nowhere. . . . Which way you heading from here?"

Fontana was quiet for a long minute, eyes half shut, scarred face expressionless. South meant Marissa and the sort of life he'd never had, only dreamed of. To the west lay Santa Fe and all of the loneliness and drudgery and danger that went with wearing a lawman's badge.

But could he live like other men? Or was he so filled with bitter memories and marked by the past that inner peace was a thing never to be a part of him? He could hope for such, strive to find it, but in his heart he knew it wasn't possible. It was not his way of life. Voluble little Curry had pegged it right—he was one of those *jaspers* who had to do the job. He smiled crookedly.

"Hadn't quite made up my mind but now I reckon you've helped me do it."

The lawman looked puzzled. "Me?"

"Yeh. Going on west to Santa Fe. Got a star waiting for me there."

K AE H J